ISBN 0-9760769-2-6
First Printing 2004
Cover art and design by Anne M. Clarkson

Published by:
Dare 2 Dream Publishing
A Division of Limitless Corporation
Lexington, South Carolina 29073
Find us on the World Wide Web
.http://www.limitlessd2d.net.

Printed in the United States of America and the UK by

Lightning Source, Inc.

III

~Buried Prejudices~

By Larisa

A low keening wail echoed in the small-darkened space, dampness seeped into chilled bones long ago to leave them aching for warmth. The sound of dripping moisture tapped from where it fell to the filthy bricks that covered the floor. The stench of human waste and decomposing bodies hung so thick in the air that breathing was hard and labored. No light was able to reach the subterranean prison, only the murky shadows of objects laying about the floor. A constant scrapping noise and small whimpers were her only companions now that she was the last survivor. Her friend had been tossed back down into the darkness days ago, so badly beaten that within hours, her body drained the last of it's essence into the cracks between the clay bricks. She didn't know if her time would come, to finally find peace in death or she would be left to suffer the unknown.

The creature that on occasion threw food and water down hadn't been there in what she could only figure in her muddled mind as to be a week. At this point, her mind was no longer hers, voices, screams, wails and the repeating cackle of the creatures laugh reverberated in her ears. She had no idea how long she had been down there, nor did she know how she came about being a prisoner. She had lost so much of herself in the dark that she no longer knew her name. Searching on the floor, she found the thin piece of rib bone that she had been using to dig in the damp dirt with. Moving the pile of human bones to the side, she searched with filthy hands for the hole she had been digging in the wall. She had found the spot while leaning against the wall the bricks were deteriorating. With the help of the bones from ones who came before her, she started scraping at the surface.

Time was not in this place, the way she measured time was by how far she tunneled each day. The soil that she pulled away from the tunnel she pushed against a far wall where, when the creature came for them, it couldn't be seen in the dark shadows. When she wasn't alone, they ate what they could of the dirt and bugs found within. If not, they would have perished long ago from starvation. She felt like a small mole in the dark, her eyes had adjusted after time, and now she was able to see somewhat in the blackness of her prison. Her hearing was also more acute from being in a place that had no sound except for the drip of moisture that was no longer heard. She jumped when she felt the vibration above her head, he was back. Quickly covering the hole with the bones and her friend's body, she crawled to a corner and hunched down to await her future.

A rope came down and dangled in front of her, a deep guttural voice told her to wrap the rope around her chest and tie it. She did this with trembling hands and waited, the rope grew taught as she came out from the darkness and into the bright sunlight. Her eyes slammed closed and a keening noise came from her throat. The cold wind chilled her naked body as it blew hard against her. She felt rough hands yank the rope from around her and force her forward. On weak stumbling legs, she moved forward under the forceful hand of her captor. With a shove from behind, she felt the ground meet her face. The crispness of dried leaves crackled against her face for brief moments before she felt hands bring her up to her knees. A large hand grabbed her dirt-matted hair at the base of her neck and pulled her head back. A sharp pain pierced her vagina as the man forced himself into her; she left her mind drift off to another world while he raped her

4

body. Traveling back to a time when she was safe in her mothers arms, the scent of cinnamon hung in the warm kitchen as she ate cookies and drank hot cocoa, the twinkling laugh of her younger sister as she ran around the table after the family dog. She could hear her mother sing a melody that reminded her of the luscious green lands of her mother's home country. It was that melody, which played in her head now to drown out the grunts that came from the man as he slammed into her. Long moments went by until she felt her body crash to the ground, squinting through an eye; she looked around to see the trees bare of leaves and the dryness of the soil around her. Off in the distance, she could hear the faint sounds of traffic, and the bark of a dog. She knew that civilization was close by but they would never know that she was there. A loud thud came to her straining ears and then a gasp from her cracked lips when her ribs were kicked by a heavy booted foot. A low click and then the fiery pain lanced across her back as yet another slice was inflicted across her filthy infected flesh. She knew from experience that it would soon fester and make her pray for death. Time was running out for her, she had five slashes to her skin now, one more and her death was guaranteed. It was his way and nothing had changed in the time she had been held as his captive.

She woke to the darkness of her prison; her body ached and felt raw. Reaching a hand down between her legs, she felt the stickiness of her blood coating the insides of her thighs. Degradation was something that had left her a long time ago, now it was part of her existence. Searching the floor around her, she found a bottle of water and a plastic bag with a half-eaten sandwich in it. Saving the water, she ate the sandwich in two bites and had to calm her stomach so as not to expel the foreign matter. After she was sure that her body would not rebel, she found her digging tool and went to work on her tunnel. She would continue to dig until she was free, even if freedom came from her death.

***

A tall dark woman dressed in a charcoal Armani suit with

a bright white dress shirt walked back and forth in front of a wall covered in pictures of missing women. The pictures started in the year 1982 until present time, she had figured out with the help of the other agents, witnesses and family members, that two women a month were taken from various places. No remains had ever been recovered in all the years, but deep down Jericho knew that they were all dead. What troubled her was where their remains could be hidden after so many years and never been discovered. Taking a seat in the chair in front of her desk, FBI Director Jericho Chamaune rubbed her tired eyes and looked down at the folders cluttering her desk. The pictures on the wall had nothing to do with the files she had been looking at earlier, they were cases pending trials and sentencing. The wall as she had started calling it was a hobby of hers, after so many years of not having a clue as who the perp was; some of the cases had been closed. Others still had agents or other agencies looking into them but she knew that they would end up the same way. She knew that all the woman shared similar traits. Dark hair and eyes looked back at her, some with green or hazel but they all had the same type of face, young, innocent background.

Pulling her long dark hair off her neck, she let her head rest against the back of her chair, swinging her feet up onto the edge of her desk; she crossed her ankles and let her ice blue eyes close. Even behind her eyelids, the faces haunted her. "Someday I will find you, someday." She came from her musings when a throat cleared in the doorway.

"I have your new Princess?" A deep throaty laugh came from the Agent who was tossing yet another folder on to the huge mess. "Another picture for your wall just came in this morning." His deep brown eyes raked a path across his boss as she relaxed in her chair. He had always been attracted to her, but knew that unless he got a sex change, he never had a chance in hell with her. Moreover, there was the little thing about being Co-workers, being his boss and his wife. "New suit Rico looks good but the cowboy boots..." He left the rest unsaid; it was a long-standing topic of her choice in footwear.

Her ice blue eyes flitted over his bulging gut and then down to his chocolate colored loafers. "At least I know what's on my feet, since when do brown loafers fit with a black suit?"

"Damn dog ate my black shoes, tore the insoles out of them. Any way, that file is from Texas. A college student at Texas A&M came up missing almost 7 months ago. They wanted us to take a look at it and see if anything popped up."

"Why didn't they put this into VICAP, or call us. Any leads on her are so old that not even Dion Warwick's psychics can help us or her."

"Aren't they in jail or something? Anyway, I've got work to do unlike other people I know."

"Go to Hell Stan, I have plenty of work." She yelled to him then mumbled the last statement to herself. "Not like I'm going to do it." Pulling the file that Stan had brought closer to her, she flipped it open and then slid the picture to the side. Skimming the content of the official report read just like some of the others.

MacDonaill, Shawna Brennan
DOB: May 22, 1971
Brown hair, green eyes, 5ft5, 120lb
Full time student Texas A&M, Major Linguistics
Reported missing by dorm mate Melissa Matthes, last seen on the morning of Oct. 4 2002.

It went on with the basics of checking friends and family members, old boyfriends, employers and local hospitals. After investigating her disappearance for three months, the case was put aside. Pulling the picture from her desk, Rico's breath caught in her chest. The eyes of Shawna held her captivated; she could drown in their sea green pools. Her heart pounded in her chest painfully as she looked at the shoulder length dark hair with blonde highlights, the bangs dropping over one finely arched dark brow giving her a seductive aura. Moving from behind her desk with picture in hand, she moved one of the older ones from the wall and placed Shawna's where she could see it from her desk. Taking her seat, she sat down and stared at the 8X10 picture. When her eyes began to blur, she tore her eyes from the picture, picked up the phone and called her assistant.

"Get me the investigating officer on the MacDonaill case out of Texas A&M campus." She hung up the phone and waited for it to ring back. Grabbing a legal pad and pen, she stacked files so that she would have a clean spot to write. The second the phone rang, she snatched it up.

"FBI Director Chamaune."

"Ya wanted to know about that MacDonaill case?"

"I just got the file today, what can you tell me?"

"Not much Ma'am." His thick Texas drawl made it hard for her to understand him. "Her dorm mate got a hold of us a couple days after she went missin, thought she was stayin with her girlfriend. We all checked with her ands she was back home in Boston with her parents at the time. We found Miss. MacDonaill's backpack near a tree along with her coat and laptop case."

"What about her laptop, was it ever found?"

"No Ma'am, we figured that someone stole that. Probably using it for schoolwork or hocked it. What confused the hell outta us, was we found her shoes in the parking lot. Why would she leave expensive Nike cross trainers and then we thought that maybe she lost them when she was abducted?"

"It's a possibility, by the way, what's your name?"

"Officer Gaines, sorry Ma'am I was kinda shocked to hear from ya'll so soon."

"It's all right. Did you put up posters or anything like that; contact the newspapers and TV stations?"

"Yes Ma'am, still have posters around campus and the town."

She knew she had hit a dead end, the Texas officials had done everything that they could. Now it was up to her to try to solve the puzzle. She just wished she had one piece to start with or that they had contacted her sooner.

"Did Shawna have any enemies or anything like that, maybe an argument with someone?"

"Nope, everything checked out, didn't get no ransom note either. Ya know she's the only one ta ever just disappear from around here."

"Thank you, I appreciate your help and if I find out anything, I'll let you know."

"If we get anything new, I'll do the same and let ya all know ASAP."

Feeling like she had no more knowledge than what she had in the file, she decided to call it a day. It was Friday and she really didn't feel like hanging around the office. She collected the file, pulled the picture off the wall and dropped both of them into her briefcase, locked her office door and went down the busy hallway to the staircase.

****

Hitting the button on her keychain, she heard the three beeps of her car alarm and then the headlights flashed on and off signaling that it was disarmed. Her Blazer was safe in the garage for the building but she didn't like to take chances with someone ripping it off. Insurance rates were bad enough since she always seemed to have to report bullet holes or other damages done to her Blazer. At times, she felt like she was paying the insurance rates that a sixteen year-old male paid. Driving the hour to her house in the Virginia countryside was worth the stressful drive. She owned 265 acres off Rt. 9 in Loudon County, two miles off the road. Her cabin style house stood surrounded by huge trees, and behind it was another smaller house that her mother lived in. She had bought the place to have peace and quiet after a long day in the city of Tyson's Corner where the FBI office was located. Pulling through the heavy metal gate at the entrance, she headed up the dirt and gravel driveway to her house. Pulling up to the double garage door, she left her Blazer sit there. She hardly ever pulled it into the garage for the simple fact that there was no room. For a hobby, she refurnished antiques on one side and on the other sat her vintage Indian Chief motorcycle.

As she climbed down from her truck, she saw her mother on the riding lawnmower. She couldn't help but grin at the way her eccentric mother was dressed, she wore a huge straw hat with dryer sheets hanging off the brim, a big cigar burning in her mouth and a flannel shirt and coveralls, they were her normal yard work attire. Behind the large tractor was a black and white pygmy nanny goat running after her screaming 'Maaa' the whole way. Her mother was by fair the most abnormal woman she knew, and when seen together, the only thing they shared in looks were the ice blue eyes. Her mother's height being only five-foot-five and her being an even six foot had her coming right up to her chest. She had chestnut colored hair with grey streaking thru at the temples and her Irish brogue still strong after nearly 40 years in the States.

Going into her house, she dropped her briefcase on the antique table near the door, tossed her suit jacket over the back of a chair and went into the large country style kitchen for a beer. Wandering through the house, she striped out of her clothes on the way to her bedroom. The master bedroom was decorated in light blues and silver. The large queen sized bed was one hundred years old; she had refinished it years ago and found matching amour and chest of drawers to go with it. Pulling a pair of boxer shorts and faded FBI t-shirt from a drawer, she redressed and went into her office. Besides her PC and desk, she had every PC Dungeons &Dragons game that ever came out; she was a game addict and saved an hour a day to play. Her mother told her she was nothing but a 6ft kid and it showed by the Spiderman on the front of her boxers.

"Jericho are ya playin that damn game again?" Her mother yelled from the kitchen. "I swear ya gonna go blind one of these days lookin at those little peoples on the screen." She came up behind her daughter and placed a hand on her shoulder. "You're home early today, got bored at work?"

"I couldn't concentrate, plus its Friday."

"And ya were a wantin ta play your game. I'm making stuffed cabbage for supper, so don't be playin until mornin."

Rico couldn't help but grin at her mother; she knew damn well if her mother didn't cook for her, she would either starve or survive on microwave dinners. She was just about to go back to her game when she heard the pitter-patter of hooves running down the hardwood floor of the hallway, then the yelling of Maaa came seconds before the little goat came in to nudge her leg.

"Go find your Mama; she's making stuffed cabbage for us." She said to the golden-eyed goat and chuckled as she took off running towards the kitchen. "Didn't want a dog or cat, had to have a goat." She shook her head when she heard her mother talking to the little animal.

***

Wet dirt fell down upon sore shoulders and arms; she knew she had to be close to the surface, as the dirt was getting wetter by the inch. She didn't know if she would be able to continue at the pace she was doing, her hands were sore and bleeding, her fingernails ragged and torn from prying rocks loose. She had dug the tunnel upward at an angle to keep it from caving in to much on top of her, as she worked forward, she pushed the dirt down past her body and now she could only move forward. She was about to give up when, a clump of dirt fell into her face and then a stream of light shone down on her from above. A burst of energy came from the knowledge that she was free, using her feet, she dug into the sides of the tunnel and pushed herself up towards the light. In minutes, she had pushed through the hole and was now lying on the ground beneath the setting sun. Slowly she opened her eyes and let them adjust to the dimming light, she looked around and knew at once she wasn't anywhere near Texas. After resting for a few minutes, she got to her knees and crawled away from the tunnel. Knowing that she would not be completely free and not knowing when the creature would show up, she got to her feet and started stumbling towards the trees ahead of her. For hours, she walked towards the sound of traffic that she heard off in the distance. Her feet cut and bleeding from stepping on rocks and branches, sharp pains shooting through her legs from exhaustion and the humming sound in her ears. She was ready to collapse when bright lights panned across her and then went past; she had made it to a road. Stumbling to the edge, she started walking towards more lights coming towards her. The blare of horns and flashing of high beams blinded her; she fell to her knees on the ground and rolled into the ditch totally exhausted. Sleep over came her, leaving her to sleep deeply amongst trash and beer cans.

***

Rico was sitting at the kitchen table drinking coffee and going over the files that she had brought home from work. She came to the MacDonaill file and pulled it open to stare down at the picture of Shawna, her heart started pounding again and sweat broke out on the palms of her hands. She had the weirdest feeling that Shawna was trying to reach out to her from the picture.

"Pretty lass, she one of your missing ones?" Her mother asked over her shoulder.

"I just got it yesterday and yeah, she's missing. I get the strangest feeling when I look at her picture." She handed it to her mother and watched to see if she noticed anything about it.

"Aye she can see right to your soul with those green eyes, maybe that's what you're seein?" She handed the picture back and took a seat across from Rico. "Where's she from and what's the lass's name?"

"Texas and its Shawna MacDonaill," She raised her eyes up to meet her mothers. "She's been missing for seven months now; I think she's like the others."

"Nah, that one there is a fighter ta the bone she is. Take my word for it wee one."

***

Rt. 340 was the busiest road in Charlestown, since the racetrack had put in slot machines; the traffic was non-stop 24 hours a day. Because of the heavy traffic, the littering of the median and the sides of the road were a gold mine in aluminum cans. One old timer went out every morning to pick up the cans to turn them into the recycling plant where he got 38cents a pound. He only needed a dozen more cans and he would have collected 75 pounds that morning alone. Getting out of his old pick-up truck a few miles down Rt. 340, he pulled his stick and garbage bag from the back of his truck and started walking. As he scanned the weeds for cans, he often found other things like road kill, clothes, household items that had fallen off trucks and anything else that could be thought of. He walked down a steep embankment and stopped in his tracks, wiping the sweat from his

12

eyes, he looked again. Lying in the tall weeds was the naked body of a young woman; he got closer and pushed the weeds away from her body.

His voice thick and rough from years of smoking un- filtered cigarettes. "God child, what happened to you?" He knelt down and placed a gnarled hand against the side of her gaunt and dirty face. He could see the pulse beating against her pale flesh and the rise of her bony chest. Dropping his stick and bag, he picked her up in his arms and carried her to his truck. After placing her across the seat, he climbed in, cut across the road and headed to the hospital. His wife would never believe what he had found and he wasn't sure that he wanted to tell her.

Old Ben pulled his truck right up to the ER doors and ran into the hospital, his granddaughter was an ER nurse and he knew that she was on duty that day. Going up to the desk, he saw that one of her friends was behind it and upon seeing him; she paged his granddaughter before he could say a word. When he saw her coming through the doors that led to the trauma rooms, he didn't give her a chance to say a word before he took her hand and dragged her out to his truck.

"Bobby ya have ta help her!"

Her hazel eyes so much like his looked up at him with confusion. "Grandpa is it Granny?"

"No, I found her laying in the ditch, she looks real bad. Ya gotta help her." He pulled the door open and revealed the malnourished body of the young woman.

"Ohh Gods Grandpa! I'll be back with a gurney." She ran back to the ER and came out seconds later with a gurney and another nurse at her side. After they had her on the gurney and covered, they rushed her inside, through the doors and to the nearest trauma room. Old Ben paced the waiting room; he hoped that the woman made it, what he couldn't figure out was where she had come from or why she was in the ditch. An hour later, Bobby came out from the back and dropped into a chair next to her Grandpa. She gripped his hand and gave him a warm smile.

"She's going to make it."

"Thank God." He said and wiped a tear from his wrinkled cheek. "Was she…ya know?"

"Yeah Grandpa, she was raped. Who ever had her didn't want her to survive; she was so dehydrated that if you hadn't found her she would have died. The sheriff said that he'll come by tonight to talk to you." She gave him a hug and kissed his cheek. "You're a hero Grandpa." She chuckled at the blush that covered his sun-darkened skin. "Better get home before Granny sends out the national guard to look for you."

"That's all I need, thanks Bobby. Ya'll let me know how she's doing."

"You bet I'll talk to you later."

Hours later, green eyes forced themselves open to see the dim light coming in from under a wooden door, the beeping sounds of machines could be heard next to the bed. The young woman turned her aching head to see the machine and an IV stand with a bag hanging from it. Bringing her hand up to her face, she noticed the IV line running into the top of her hand and a plastic admittance band around her wrist.

"You're awake? That's good." A deep voice came from the doorway. The young woman took one look at the bearded face and screamed out a keening sound. Falling from the bed, she crouched in the corner and continued to make terrible sounds. The male nurse flipped the light on and jumped back when the phone from the table flew at him. "Calm down, I won't hurt you." He tried to get closer and had to dodge a bedpan flying towards him. Giving up, he left the room to look for a doctor. The low keening noise continued and then grew louder when a tall doctor came into the room with the male nurse. They tried to approach her from different sides but were forced back when she started howling and kicking out with her feet. "See what I mean Doc, she's nuts." The male nurse said of the woman. "Should I call the head doc?"

"What is going on here?" Bobby asked from the doorway.

"She's gone nuts, we were just going to try and get a hold of her." The male nurse said as he walked closer to the cringing woman.

"Get OUT! Both of you, can't you see she's afraid of men!" She grabbed the male nurse by his arm and pulled him back. "She's a rape victim you dumb ass, she's afraid of men and

14

you two idiots are not making it any better by stalking her." She whispered to the doctor. "I'll take care of her, now get out." She faced both men with her hands firmly planted on her hips, pointing at the door, she hissed at them. "Out!" Once they were gone, she sat on the edge of the bed and waited for the woman to calm down.

"It's OK, I won't hurt you. What's your name?" She ran her hand through her honey colored curly hair and sighed. "I promise no one will hurt you." She sat for long minutes looking into the terrified green eyes; there was only one person she knew that could possible help. Her friend could tame a wild animal with one look; she knew that she could handle a small-terrified woman.

***

"This had better be good or else!" Jericho barked over the phone.

"Believe me its good! I need your wild animal skills here at the hospital ASAP!"

"Come on Bobby, what are you guys doing over there treating wolves?"

"Nope, Grandpa found a naked woman laying in the ditch this morning. She woke up a few minutes ago and is huddled in the corner and making the most God awful noises I've ever heard."

"And you want me to do what?"

"Rico, she's a rape victim and she looked like she had been buried alive."

Jericho's heart started beating out of her chest, her eyes closed as she tried to concentrate on calming her racing pulse. "I'll be there in fifteen minutes, don't let anyone near her OK?"

"Thanks Rico, and I won't, I'll guard the door with my body."

Jericho threw a pair of faded jeans on over her boxers, pulled her boots on and ran for her Blazer, she didn't know why she was doing this but she had the strangest feeling. Pulling the

15

flashing blue light from the floorboard, she placed it on her dash and turned it on. One of the benefits not being law enforcement was being able to clear the roads with just a flashing light. Skidding around the corner of the hospital, she parked her truck in the ER patient lot and ran through the side door. She was half way down the hall when she saw Bobby sitting in a chair outside of a room.

"OK Bobby, where's the wild animal?"

"She's in here, she's still making funny noises and she bites really hard. Just ask the manly man at the front desk."

Her blue eyes grew wide. "She bit someone and you want me to go in there?"

"You're the big bad FBI Director; I think you can fight off a tiny little blondish woman."

Jericho's shoulders slumped; she shook her head and gave Bobby a crocked grin. "If she bites me, I'm biting you back, got me?"

"Sure but then you'll have to fight my wife." She squeezed Jericho's shoulder and grinned. "Good luck Rico."

"You know I'm not Xena."

"Yep, besides that's not Gabrielle in there, that one makes Callisto look sane!" She opened the door for her friend and stepped back.

Jericho stepped in to the room and waited to see what would happen, she heard soft whimpers coming from the farthest corner. Stepping around the bed, she sat down on the edge across from where the woman was huddled in the corner with her arms wrapped around her head. She didn't quite know what to do, so she cleared her voice. A low growling noise came from the corner, she felt shivers go up her back from the noise. Then it changed to a low voice that sang softly.

Codladh fada,
Codladh domhain.
Éirigh! Amharc síos
Aldebaran.

Jericho sang the last part in a deep clear voice and waited.

Siúil liom tríd an réalta dearg.
Deireadh, deireadh an turas.

16

Réaltóg, réaltóg dearg.

Aldebaran.

Her voice was soft and low, sounding like a purr. "I won't hurt you." A dark head slowly moved up to reveal sea green eyes, Jericho's breath caught in her chest at the site before her. After composing herself, she whispered Shawna and saw sparks erupt in the woman's eyes. "I'm here to help you Shawna." She eased off the edge of the bed and kneeled on the floor, reaching out a hand, she offered it to her. "Take my hand Shawna." Jericho turned her head when she heard the whoosh of the door behind her and a doctor came into the room. She heard the keening wail and then a body flew into her arms and shook like a leaf. Wrapping one arm around Shawna, she shot a glare at the doctor and pointed to the door. "Get out!"

"Who the hell are you; you have no right being in here!" He yelled back at her.

"Fuck you asshole!" She growled, pulled her wallet out and showed him her badge. "This says I do; now unless you want the FBI delving into your personal life, I suggest that you get out!"

She picked Shawna up in her arms and held her close to her body, thin arms wrapped around her neck in a strangle hold as her face pressed in to the side of Jericho's neck. Moving slowly to the bed, she tried to get her to let go.

"It's OK, just lay down and let me cover you up, you need to rest now." She felt the extremely emancipated body relax and let go of her neck. She pulled the covers up to her chest and ran soothing fingers across her gaunt cheek. "Sleep now wee one." She moved towards the door and peeked out to see Bobby and her wife Bridget standing in the hallway. "Pssst hey come here a minute you two." She moved more into the hallway and felt a body latch onto her from behind. "I have a slight problem here…she won't let go."

"Huh?" Bridget asked as she looked at her friend and then to her wife, her caramel colored eyes blinked with confusion. "Who won't let go of you?"

"Her names Shawna, I tamed her now she's hanging onto the back of me." She pointed down to the small hands wrapped around her waist. "Come on Doc B. can you sign her out to me and have your beautiful and gifted wife come and check on her once a day?" She gave them a pleading look. "She's one of my cases and she's in danger here."

"Shit Rico, why didn't you say that. Give me a minute and I'll take care of it." Bridget took off down the hall towards the main desk.

"Bobby can you get the meds and anything else she'll need for the night?"

"I sure hope to god you know what you're doing."

"If she escaped from her capture, then he's looking for her." She flinched when the thin arms tightened around her.

Bobby's eyes grew wide. "I never thought of that! I'll be right back, go take care of Shawna."

Jericho moved back into the room, as soon as she turned around she found her arms full of Shawna; she didn't know what else to do but hold her and sing the Gaelic song to her. Before she could finish the second verse, she felt Shawna relax against her, her breathing became deep and even in sleep. Picking her up in her arms, she sat down on the bed and rocked her while continuing to sing softly near her ear.

A while later, she saw Bridget's dark head peek through the door and then Bobby's above her. She nodded for them to come in.

"She's sleeping, am I all set to take her?"

"Yeah, all set. Bobby has all the stuff you'll need for the next couple of days."

"I'll come by tomorrow and check on her. Will you be home?"

Jericho nodded her head and then stood up. "Can you take that out to my truck for me?"

***

The ride home for them was something that shocked Jericho, Shawna woke after five minutes on the road, her green eyes showed panic until she saw Jericho. She moved as close as she could to the tall woman and lay her head on her thigh with

18

her hands gripping her shirt. She didn't move until the Blazer stopped and very carefully looked out of the windshield.

"It's OK, this is my home you're safe here."

Moving out of the Blazer, Jericho held out her hand to her but found thin arms wrapped around her neck. It seemed that she would be carrying the small woman around. After going into the house, she didn't know what to do with her. She had spare rooms but none of them had any beds in them, she never had guests so she never thought of getting extra beds. Carrying her to her bedroom, she laid her down and then covered her up with the thick comforter.

Caressing a gaunt and bruised cheek, she looked into tired green eyes. "Are you hungry, I can get you something to eat?"

"Please." Shawna said with a raspy voice.

After heating up what was left of the stuffed cabbage, she filled a glass with milk and took it into her bedroom. Pulling a tray from under the bed, she placed everything on it and placed it across Shawna's lap. Pulling utensils from her pocket along with a napkin, she handed them to her.

"I'll be back in a little while, if you need anything just give a yell OK?" Shawna nodded her head and started to eat like a starving animal. "Slow down or you'll get sick." She placed a large hand over Shawna's smaller one to slow her down. "If you're still hungry after this I can get you something else." She knew from the condition that she was in that she wouldn't be able to eat even a small portion of the food; her stomach was probably so small that it couldn't hold too much without rebelling. "My bathroom is through that door if you need it." She then left her to eat and went to the kitchen to call her mother.

"Mama I have a house guest that I would like you to help me with tomorrow." She explained about the phone call from Bobby. In addition, how her Grandpa had found Shawna. Her mother couldn't believe that the woman in the picture that she had only seen that morning was with Jericho. It was a miracle she just knew it. "I'll see you tomorrow Mama." She hung up the phone and went in to check on her guest. When she stepped into the room, Shawna was on her side and holding onto her pillow with both arms. Moving closer, she covered her up and took the tray back to the kitchen. Grabbing a pillow from the hall closet, she went to the couch and lay down. Her eyes dropped closed and sleep over took her.

***

Shawna fought with her restraints; the heaviness about her body was stifling. Tossing and turning, she kicked outward and felt chilled airbrush against her bare skin. The darkness had closed in around her and held her in place, the sound of a deep gruff voice echoed in her ears.

"Whores, allllll of you are whores! Impureness runs through your wombs, you are not of the one true God! Herr Fuehrer!"

She felt him slam into her and cuss her origins with each thrust of his hips. The stench from his body made her gag; it reminded her of wet earth and death. Filthy hands wrapped around her neck and pulled her head back when he climaxed inside of her. A howl of rage burst past his lips, he flung her to the ground and then kicked her so hard that she slid over the edge of the hole and downward. As she lay on her stomach with her back burning from his most recent cut to her flesh, she felt a hot wetness splash down onto her. This creature that had her, acted more like an animal than she felt. After each time he rapped one of them, he urinated on them before slamming the door closed. But the wetness felt different this time, it was cold and chilling.

***

Jericho came up off the couch with the first scream; her heart slamming into her chest had her panting for air. Running a hand across her face, she listened for another sound. It came as running feet down the hallway. Before she could untangle herself from the coffee table and couch, Shawna ran past her and out the front door.

"Son of a bitch!" She let out as she jumped over the table and ran for the front door. It had started to downpour at some point; the wind whipped her long hair into her face. Brushing back the wet hair, she scanned the yard for the small woman. As a flash of lightning brightened the sky, she saw her on her knees in the center of the yard. Walking slowly up to her, she whispered her name and reached out a hand to her shoulder. "Let's go back inside, it's cold out here." She flinched when crazed green eyes locked with hers. "Shawna, I won't hurt you. It's Jericho, remember?" *Of course, she doesn't remember you dumbass, you never told her who you were.* Stepping closer, she lifted her chin and looked deeply into her eyes. "Look at me Shawna, I won't hurt you." She felt a small cold hands grip her forearm and wrist. Shawna ran her fingers across her muscled forearm and then looked up into her silvery eyes.

"Cold, so cold." Were the only words she said, before she passed out and fell into Jericho's arms.

She carried her into the house and right to the bathroom, while holding her; she turned the shower on and adjusted the water. Sitting her on the edge of the bathtub, she removed the wet hospital gown and let out a low moan when she saw the scars, bruises and fresh wounds on her frail body. Holding onto her with one hand, she stripped out of her own clothes and then lifted her in her arms to stand beneath the warm water. After a few minutes, she made the water a little hotter until she felt the small body stop shivering. Brushing the wet hair back from her face, she was able to see just how gaunt she really was.

Her heart broke in her chest and then anger took over to rush through her body. She would never understand how another human could do this to someone. She vowed to herself that she would get the animal that did this and make sure that he never hurt anyone ever again. Shutting the water off and climbing from the tub, she went to her room and laid Shawna down on the bed. She removed the wet bandages and upon seeing her body shiver again, she slid in beside her and pulled her close to her own body. Small thin arms wrapped around her waist, a wet head pressed against her breasts and then soft snores came from parted lips.

Jericho lay with her in her arms for what seemed ages before she fell back to sleep. When the sun came through the window to shine in her eyes a low groan rumbled in her chest. She was used to being up before the break of dawn, but after the night before, she was exhausted and felt achy. She felt warm moist air graze her neck and a soft murmur in her ear. Shawna was spooned against her back and holding on for dear life. She was about to ease out from the bed when her mother peeked into the   room.

"Mama." She whispered and motioned for her to come closer. "Will   you   watch   her   until   I   get   dressed?"

Blue eyes met for an instant before a small smile graced Marie's lips. "Go ahead wee one, I'll watch her." She sat on the edge of the bed while her daughter went to the bathroom to shower and get dressed. She brushed back the shaggy streaked hair of the small woman and held back a groan. The pale face looked so frail and China delicate, the skin, thin enough to see the blood rushing through the veins. She was reminded of the holocaust survivors from WWII; she knew that Jericho would do everything she could to find the person who had done this. She also knew that this small woman would come to mean the world to her lonely child. After her father dying in a trucking accident and her brother Samuel dying from a rare blood disease, Jericho never had anyone in her life but her. She worried at times about Jericho and her hermit type life but thought that it was because of seeing the horrors of the world that kept her alone. Now, a small woman with sea green eyes and the strength to survive a living nightmare   would   change   all   that.

Marie went back to her own house to get some things that Jericho would need later that day, she left worrying about her daughter trying to make something to eat. She knew she could use the microwave but when it came time to use the stove it became down right scary. She chuckled to herself when she remembered Rico, as she called her, tried to make a roasted chicken. When she pulled it from the oven, it looked more like a dried up pigeon than a Purdue oven roaster. Folding the sweatshirt and jeans up, she found a pair of Tennis shoes that she knew Shawna would be able to wear. Thinking for a second, she pulled one of Rico's old jackets from the closet and added that to the small pile. It maybe the month of May, but it was a cold month this year and the weather changed so drastically from one minute to the next that she wondered if they would have a summer that year. Satisfied with her scavenger hunt, she headed back to Rico's house with her goat in tow.

***

Shawna had woke to find herself alone in a big warm bed, the sun warming her skin as it came through the window. Easing her body under the flannel sheets a small smile came to her face with the memory of a warm gentle body holding her. The thoughts in her head were all jumbled, but one thing she remembered above all else was the deep throaty purr of a woman's voice and ice blue eyes. She felt very safe with her and for once in her life since being kidnapped felt rested and warm. Her legs ached and numerous other areas of her body but she knew that would go away with time. She was free and would never look back. Swinging her legs over the side of the bed a bit of dizziness claimed her, taking a deep breath, she got to her feet and stood looking around the large bedroom. It gave the feeling of being cherished when she saw the antique furniture so lovingly cared for. Feeling a slight chill to her skin, she saw a t-shirt lying across the foot of the bed. Bringing it to her nose, she picked up the scent of a light musky perform and another scent of spices. Once she was dressed, she cautiously made her way to where she heard music. Coming to the door of the kitchen, she saw the tall woman pouring a cup of coffee. From the width of her back and shoulders, she knew that she was a strong person and could be very dangerous. But in her arms, she felt nothing but a deep tenderness and a little bit of fright.

"Morning," She mumbled past dry lips. "Can I have some coffee?" She asked while still hiding in the doorway.

Rico turned slowly, she didn't want to startle her and have her run outside screaming again. A small smile came to her lips when she saw her dressed in her t-shirt. Pointing to a chair, she reached for another cup from the hangers.

"Have a seat, you want cream and sugar?"

"Please."

Rico couldn't help but chuckle at her politeness, not even her Agents said 'please' to her. After setting the cup in front of

23

her, she took her own seat and sipped at the hot brew. She found herself watching the small woman and felt a protectiveness developing towards her. She looked towards the side door when she heard tiny hoof beats on the deck and a strangled Maaaa.

"You stay out here, Rico has company and she doesn't need ya running through the house."

"Mama you can let her in, she'll just stand out there and cry if you don't."

Shawna looked like she was ready to bolt; Rico placed a hand on top of hers and calmed her with her voice. "It's my Mama; she lives in the house out back." Shawna looked at the older version of Rico, the eyes held her and twinkled with a gentleness that only a mother has.

"What do you two want for breakfast? I brought fresh goats milk over earlier." She cocked an eyebrow at the shiver that went through Rico. "I know you hate goat's milk, don't seem ta mind that I cook with it now do ya."

"That's 'cuz I don't know when you use it." She looked at the smiling face of Shawna. "She tries to make me eat that healthy stuff." She jumped in her chair when a tiny little head ran into her knees under the table. "Jed you little shit stop that. Mama your goats chewing on my pocket."

"You know what she wants, so gives it ta her. It's your fault anyway."

Shawna looked under the table and was met by a tiny little head tilting sideways and looking at her with a golden eye. A small 'Maa' rumbled from its mouth and little teeth showed when a fuzzy lip raised. Rico held out an atomic fireball candy and waited until it was wet and sticky from a long wet tongue before she popped it into Jed's mouth.

"You do that on purpose you little shit." Getting up to wash her hand, she gave her Mother a smirk. Looking over her shoulder, she saw Shawna lean down and rest her forehead against the goats. She nudged her mother and nodded towards the table.

"You're a spoiled baby aren't cha?" Shawna said in a low voice.

"That there be Jericho's evil dog, or Jed fer short. Never

24

could understand her gettin a pygmy goat." She cast a glance at her daughters dropped jaw.

"Mama, I did not get a goat, you got her. You just like blaming me for her turning out like a dog."

"I knows wee one, just like ta tease ya is all. Who else can get away with it aye?" She cast a look at Shawna and pointed. "Except maybe wee bit there." She slapped Rico on her shoulder and told her to put her backside in a chair before she kicked it.

After eating a huge breakfast, Rico left Shawna with her mother and went to her office to make some phone calls to the local police department to get their reports on Shawna and to find the exact location that she had been found. After spending three hours on the phone, she rubbed her sore ear and went into the kitchen to get a cup of coffee. Looking out the window over the sink, she saw Shawna now dressed in the clothes Marie had given her and sitting in the grass with Jed curled up beside her. She looked so small and lost sitting there and she wondered what was going through her head at that moment. Thinking back on the night before and the terrified look on her face as she stood in the cold downpour, brought shivers to Rico's body. She could only imagine what she endured while being held captive. Knowing that in the very near future she would have to question her did not make her feel any better. Maybe she could get her mother to help with that area, Marie had a way of calming the tides when it came to frightened children and that's what Shawna reminded her off. Picking up the keys to her Blazer, she walked out the side door and over to where Shawna was sitting, crouching down on her haunches she spoke in a low tone.

"I have to go arrange some stuff; I'll be back in a few hours." She felt the terror come over Shawna and reached out a hand to her. "Mama will be here with you, my cell phone number is by the phone in the kitchen if you need me."

"Thank you for everything." She said as tears filled her green eyes. "Can I call my Mom and let her know I'm OK?"

"Yeah, you can give her the phone number if you want." She caressed her cheek and then went to tell her mother where she was going. She knew that who ever it was that had taken Shawna wouldn't be able to figure out where she was by her

25

calling her mother. The security system that she had on her house and property made the Pentagon security system look like Kmart's. Every phone call was encrypted as it passed through her computer before it was sent across the phone lines and vice versa. It made caller ID units go berserk and spit out 1 900 numbers.

***

A dual wheeled truck rumbled through the open fields, mud sprayed up from the huge tires as they went around the worn path between the tumbled down buildings that had been left to fall down almost 30 years ago. Being a forgotten area and off limits to hunting made it a perfect area for what the man used it for. He hit the button on the worn Nazi youth switchblade and snickered each time the blade shot in and out of the end. Making a notch in the dashboard with the sharp end, he now had a perfect 40 hash marks. One for each woman he had taken in the surrounding area. After the one in the hole was dead, he would go out that night and get two or three more to play with. Pulling the truck up to the dirt and brush covered trap door, he got out and cleared it off and used the hoist on the back of the truck to lift it. It was made out of solid concrete and weighed more than his truck did. He had poured it himself and hauled it to this spot just for this purpose. Once it was slid over to the side, he dropped the rope into the hole and yelled down. Squinting, he tried to see movement in the darkness below.
"Whore move where I can see you!" He bellowed and when nothing happened below, he got a large heavy-duty flashlight from his truck and shinned it into the pitch black. Hitting every corner, he came up with only one body that was falling apart from decomposition. The stench made his nose and eyes water, and a gag reflex grab his innards. Shinning the light one last time, he let out a scream when he saw a little bit of light come from the base of the floor. Running to the other side of the hole, he found the tunnel exit and knew that she had some how had enough energy to dig her way out. Right then he knew that the new ones would get no food or water. If they had nothing then they would not have the strength to escape. Granted they

26

wouldn't last as long but he would replace them after they died. Checking the ground around the hole and then searching further away showed no trace as to where she had gone. Then he thought of the condition that she had been in the last time he had tried to destroy her womb and knew that she was lying out in the woods somewhere dead. After replacing the concrete slab, he got back in his truck and left his buried secret for the next batch of what he called the supreme races down fall. It was his job to rid the earth of their impurities and bring about the next super human race to over through the weak. Running a hand across the scruffy beard that he hated and drove him nuts with its itching, he tore out of the field and up onto the black topped road.

"Need to shave this off, no more disguises of who I really am." He looked into the rearview mirror to see his dark brown eyes starring crazily back at him. "Herr Fuehrer!"

**

Rico walked along the side of the road with old Ben and a sheriff's deputy, she wanted to see the exact spot that Shawna had been found at and then scan the surrounding area to see in which direction she had come from. She knew it would be useless since the heavy rains would have washed all evidence away, not only for her investigation but also for the one who had kidnapped her to begin with. If she couldn't find anything than neither could he. Dropping down to her haunches, she used a stick to push the tall weeds to the side. Nothing could be seen and all particles would have been washed away, that is if Bobby had pulled one of her normal stunts and collected evidence when she was brought into the hospital.

"Ben, has anyone other than you been in your truck since you took the woman to the hospital."

"Nope, just her, ya wanna check for evidence?"

"Yep, won't find anything out here since the weather last night." She came to her feet and looked out across the open and wooded fields. "Any idea which direction she could have come from?"

"She did have leaves and stuff stuck to her, so I was thinking that she came down from near the river."

27

Rico trained blue eyes on him. "Is there anything over there that she could have been hidden in for months without any one knowing?"

"Rico, in this area there are so many places that someone could hide an entire Marine Battalion and no one would be the wiser."

Tapping the deputy on the shoulder, she asked him if he had a large map of the area. What he produced wasn't exactly what she was looking for but it would help. Spreading it out on the hood of the cruiser, she asked Ben to show her areas that at one time had been civilized.

After a few minutes of pointing out areas, she knew that she would need the Marines to search the place.

"Where can I get a topographical map of this area?"

Ben rubbed his baldhead and squinted at the ground. "County courthouse may have one and if not there's the surveyors, they always have them for keeping track of stuff. I know they have aerial maps to, ya know shot from their helicopter." He gave her a crocked grin and raised an eyebrow. "You gonna find that bastard all on your own ain't cha?"

Her grin matched his as well as the raised brow. "And when I find him, he's gonna be sorry he was ever born. Thanks for your help, tell everyone I said hey and I'll talk to them soon." After they had parted ways, she went into town and got the maps she needed and then went into Staples Office Supply store to get an assortment of things that she would need for her one-woman manhunt. When she got home, she would call in to work and take some of her vacation that she had never used. She knew she had at least five years worth of vacation days and she was going to start using them as of the coming Monday. Going into Wal-Mart, she called her mother on her cell phone to find out what size clothes Shawna wore. She would buy her what ever she needed to feel comfortable and something's just because she thought the young woman would like them. She had never done anything like what she was doing and wondered why. The only thing that she could think of was that deep down she felt some kind of connection with Shawna.

***

Shawna wiped the tears from her cheeks after Marie told her what Rico was doing. She had only known the tall woman less than a day and she had brought her to her home, taken care of her and was buying her clothes.

"Why is she doing this?" She asked Marie.

"That's just how she is and no use arguing with her either. She can throw up a wall that a bulldozer couldn't knock down." Marie knew damn well that her daughter had never done such a thing but had an idea as to why she had done a 180-degree turn. "Ya knows, she will do what ever she has ta be done ta catch the bastard."

Green eyes locked with blue for long moments before they dropped down to look at damaged hands and nails.

"But why, I mean isn't that what the police are for?"

"Shawna, Rico is a Director for the FBI. She can do anything she wants and no one can say a word."

"I didn't know I just knew that people back away from her in a hurry."

"Ohh what did my wee one do this time?" She rolled her pale blue eyes and let out a small laugh. "Must have scared a doctor or two yesterday." She placed a cup of herbal tea heavy on the honey and a few pills in front of Shawna and sat down. "Can you remember anything from yesterday?"

"It's all so blurry, I was scared and confused. I'm still that way…scared." She took the pills and washed them down with the tea, she had been eating small amounts of food since breakfast and was feeling better, but her body had been neglected for so long, that it would take weeks if not months for her to become completely healthy. "How did Rico know I was at the hospital?" Marie told her about how she had been found and all that led up to her being brought to Rico's home. "Do ya have someone that you want to know that you're OK?"

"I tried calling my Mom, but I got no answer." Tears came to her eyes. "I don't even know if she still lives where I called." Marie stood up, moved around the table, and took her into her arms.

29

"Does she have a job, or maybe you have another relative you can call?"

"My sister lives with her; at least she did before I was kidnapped. They must think I'm dead." She broke down into racking sobs and was held tighter in Marie's embrace. Marie did what she had always done when her children were hurt, she sang an old Gaelic folk song and waited for them to fall asleep.

***

Rico stopped off at the hospital and collected the small plastic bags that Bobby had placed fingernail scrapings and other small bits of evidence in. Since Shawna had been a rape victim, those specimens had been sent off to the lab and Bobby would forward the findings directly to Rico when they came in. She often asked Bobby to join the FBI and become one of their technicians and work on cases and get paid for what she did, but was always turned down. Bobby liked being a nurse and with Bridget being the resident surgeon, they had it made. She stopped off at her favorite Chinese restaurant, picked up one of everything on the menu, and headed home. She knew that her mama would throw a fit at first but in the end, she would be thankful that she didn't have to cook. Grabbing the numerous take-out bags from the passenger seat, she went around to the kitchen door and found her mama drinking tea and reading the newspaper. Placing all the bags on the table, she grinned and shrugged her shoulders.

"I have a craving for chicken egg fu young. Where's Shawna?"

"In your bed sleeping, get everything done today?"

"And then some. Did she call her mom, I told her she could?"

"That's one of the things I wanted to talk ta ya about wee one, her mama moved away. She doesn't know how ta get a hold of her."

"I'll take care of that." She looked at her watch and saw that it was still early. "If you'll get the plates ready, I'll see if I can get a phone number for her mom."

Marie placed a hand upon her daughters arm and looked up into her blue eyes, brushing back her bangs she gave her a small smile. "You'd move heaven fer her wouldn't cha wee one?" Dark brows dropped over a straight nose, a slow grin began to form on pink lips, ending in her lopsided smile that always amused Marie. "There's my answer, now get so I can fix the plates." Filling the plates with food, she thought of the change in her daughter in the last few hours. She hoped she knew that Shawna had a long road of physical as well as emotional healing ahead of her and that the road would be bumpy as Hell for a while. The poor thing didn't even know what State she was in or how she had gotten there.

***

Being so high up on the food chain as Rico liked to describe her position in the FBI, she was able to access certain files that no one else could get at. After a few key strokes, she was into the phone company's database. Although the way she got there was illegal as Hell, she got what she needed and jumped out the back door of the security system. "Have to tell them about their little program problem." She mumbled to herself. "Writing the phone number down on a piece of paper, she took with her back out to the kitchen and placed it on the table. "I got it, it's a Dallas exchange and unlisted. She must have done that after Shawna disappeared."

"I never doubted you're hacking skills wee one."

"Mama I don't hack I…hack." She shrugged her shoulders and grinned.

"Go wake Shawn up, foods ready."

Rico gave her a funny look. "Ya changing her name for her are ya?"

"Nah, she likes Shawn better, says her mama only used Shawna when she was in trouble."

"Sounds familiar," She dodged the hand that was aimed for her ass and ran out of the kitchen. Turning the nightstand light on she looked down into the calm face of Shawn, she looked different from earlier in the day. Her skin looked a healthier color and the bruising was fading. "Now if we can get some weight on you." She whispered while running her fingers through soft hair.

"Your mama's trying." One green eye opened to connect with blue. "By the end of the week I'll weigh 200 lbs." She rolled over onto her back and stretched with a little bit of pain running through her body. She sniffed the air and grinned at Rico. "Chinese   food."

"I stopped on my way home. I got your mom's new phone number   for   you;   you   can   call   after   you   eat."

Tears formed in Shawn's eyes, it had been so long since she had spoken with her mom. She hadn't the slightest idea of what to say to her. "Thank you Rico." Rico helped her out of the bed and kept a hand on her shoulder as they walked to the kitchen. Shawn couldn't believe all the food that was on the table, it looked like enough to feed a small army. If it was seven months earlier, the food on the table would have been just a snack to her, now   a   few   mouthfuls   had   her   full.

"After you're ready to turn in tonight, I'll redress your injuries. I talked to Bobby, so I'll actually know what I'm doing."

"OK, can you tell me afterward what my back looks like? I know he was marking me somehow." She took a seat next to Marie, picked up a set of chopsticks, and decided that with the condition her hands were in that a fork would be easier to use.

Shawn had eaten more at that meal than she had since arriving at Rico's; with her stomach full and the medication she was taking to help with the infections from the numerous wounds on her body. She was fighting her eyes from closing while sitting at the table. Marie nudged Rico and motioned for her to take Shawn to bed. Lifting her from the chair, she felt her arms wrap around her neck and her face rest against her neck. It felt like the most   natural   thing   for   her   to   do.

"If you need help with her dressings give me a yell."

"Mama why don't you just come with me now, I talked to Bobby but..." She shrugged her shoulders and received a grin from   her   mother.

"OK,   is   the   stuff   in   your   bathroom?"
"Yep, and I bought some larger sterile pads for her back."

***

Shawn was sound asleep when Rico laid her on the bed, easing the Levi's down her hips, she was careful when she came to her bandaged feet. She knew that her mother had to have re-bandaged them that morning after she had left. After her clothes were removed, Rico took in the full picture of the thin body. How the skin looked like it was just draped over bones, her hips sharp and pointy and the layer of hair looking almost like fur that covered her body. It was a tell tale sign of anorexia. She felt her mother come up behind her and place her arm around her waist.

"She'll   get   better   in   time."

"I know mama; it's that I just can't believe that..."

"Shawn's a lot stronger than she looks. Let's get her dressings   changed   so   that   you   can   get   some   sleep."

When they rolled her over and removed the large bandages from her back, Marie dragged a breath through her teeth. One large S was carved on her back, one more line on the other and she would have had the SS mark of Hitler's most dangerous troop. In between the double SS was a branding of the swastika.

Tears filled Rico's blue eyes to flow over and trail down her   cheeks.   "Mama?"

"You know who to look fer now wee one. Nazi's"

***

Rico sat at her computer pulling up everything she could on the Neo Nazi movement and the SS Troops of Hitler. Saving numerous documents to a file folder, she then searched the web for articles about the prisoners of concentration camps dating from WWI all the way to WWII. Hanoi Hilton was the most famous one for our solders and numerous sites had tales from the men who were at that prison. What made her stomach turn was a web site about the Elite SS Troops of Hitler. Hundreds of pictures of the Jews, Gypsies and other nationalities that the Germans killed during Hitler's reign of terror.   Some of the pictures showed close-ups of dead prisoners at Majdanek, Auswitz, Dachau, Treblinka and Bergen-Belson. They all looked like Shawn, the walking dead. Wiping the tears from her eyes, she saved the files and shut down her computer. When she went into the kitchen, she found her mama sitting at the table reading from an old worn black book that she had never seen before. It was the Mein Kempf. Her sad eyes looked up at the tear-stained face of her daughter and offered her a small smile.

"This was your father's book; it'll help ya to understand what is going through that bastards mind." She closed it, then went to her distraught daughter, and gave her a tight hug. "Now go to Shawn, ya need sleep and she needs ya to keep the nightmares away. I'll lock up for ya" Rico nodded her head, kissed her mama's cheek and went to her bedroom. She shed her clothes and slipped in beside Shawn but left distance between their bodies. Within minutes, she joined the small woman in sleep.

***

Rico felt the bed bounce and then the covers were yanked from her body. Sitting up in bed and turned to see Shawn struggling in her sleep, low keening noises came from her chest as her hands lashed out at her invisible attacker. Placing a hand upon her shoulder, Rico spoke softly trying to calm her. When Shawn started to become more violent in her sleep, Rico had no choice but to wrap her arms around her and hold her tight to her body. Resting her head on a small shoulder, she started to sing in her mother's language. Shawn's struggles lessoned and then stopped all together. Easing up on her hold, she was not surprised when Shawn rolled into her body and snuggled her face against her breasts. They sunk in to deep sleep wrapped around each other.

Shawn woke to a warmness against her face and body, opening one eye she looked down at the firm breast at eye level. A bright blush covered her face, moving slowly away from Rico, she slipped from the bed and headed to the bathroom. After relieving herself, she felt a pulling on the skin of her back. Reaching over her shoulder, she pulled at the tape from the bandage. She held back a yelp as it pulled the hair on her back. Turning so that she could see in the mirror, she pulled the bandage off and fell to her knees with a wail. Rico jumped from the bed, ran into the bathroom, and knelt in front of Shawn. Pulling her into her arms, she held her against her chest and let her cry. "What's the matter wee bit?" She whispered close to her ear. Shawn looked up with tears falling down her cheeks.

"He's   a   Nazi."

"Yes and I will find him and make him pay." She rocked her in her arms until the tears stopped. "Shawn I need to ask you some questions, let me know when you feel strong enough to do it OK?" Placing a kiss on her tousled head, she held her for a while longer.

***

Rico was in her office delving into the FBI's data base on anything she could find on the Neo Nazi's and criminals associated with the group. After coming up with certain people, she saved the files. Going back to an article that she had found on the web, she read about the emotional problems of Adolf Hitler. Making notes on a legal pad as she read, she came to the last page and her jaw dropped open. The gist of the article said that Hitler was a homosexual that frequented a place called Mannerheim, which catered to homosexual men and their lover's. That while living in Vienna he became involved with many Jewish men and was considered a homosexual gigolo or prostitute. He later wrote in Mein Kempf that his hatred for the Jews came from their sexual perversions, the molesters, seducers and corrupters of morals. That later in life he would attack total strangers and give heated lectures and was believed to be suffering from manic psychosis. Her mind was spinning, if this nutcase that was kidnapping women was trying to pull off what Hitler had done during WWII with the Jews because of having gay Jewish lovers, could there also be missing males that could be connected to this animal. And were all the women gay or friends with gays? And how is he able to transport the women from so many different states (if they were all his victims) with out getting caught. She knew she would have to ask Shawn. She dropped her head into her hands and sighed. She was getting a migraine from all that she had read and tried to figure out.

"Are you OK?" Shawn asked from the doorway where she had been watching Rico pour over documents.

"My brain is crispy." She dropped her head onto her desk and groaned. Shawn snickered at the way she was moaning and groaning, walking into the office, she started to massage the tightness in Rico's shoulders.

"Ohhh Gods, can you keep that up for the next 40 or 50 years?"

"You'll fall asleep way before then. What were you reading, that is if you can tell me."

"It was about Hitler's hatred for the Jews and how it all came about from him being a homosexual and having sexual relations with Jewish men. I'm trying to figure out..."

"If there's a connection with what happened to me?"

Rico raised her head and looked over her shoulder into curious green eyes. "Yeah, the Neo Nazi's don't kidnap people. They like to terrorize them but there are no reports of anything other than that."

"So you're thinking that this is some kind of Psychotic person who has a thing for the Fuehrer..." She became white as a sheet; her hands trembled where they rested on Rico's shoulders. "Ohh Gods! He kept saying about impurities of my womb and not being of the one true God Herr fuehrer." Rico turned her chair around and pulled Shawn onto her lap.

"So he either thinks that Hitler is God or he thinks he's Hitler?" She leaned her head back into the chair and groaned again. "I'm so confused."

"How many women are missing that you think this animal has kidnapped?"

"Not quite sure, there's close to 500 missing that have never turned up that the FBI knows about. I can't see him kidnapping that many women and not being seen or getting caught."

"Where he had me, there were remains of other women or men down there with me." Shawn started to tremble as she spoke; tears filled her eyes to flow down her cheeks. "A woman by the name of Jeanne Holton from Washington state; was down there with me, she died a while before I escaped."

"You don't have to tell me this now; I can see that it hurts to remember."

"No, I have to get this out." She wiped the tears from her chin and gave a small smile. "I'm the only survivor; I know things that can help you catch him. I may be a little unbalanced from what I lived through but I'm alive."

"Tell me what you can; you can stop when ever you want."

***

The sun had come out with a vengeance against all living creatures, Shawn sat beneath a tree going over notes that she had taken in one of her classes. Leaning back against the tree, she closed her eyes to rest for a short while before heading for her next class. Used to having other students all around her, she didn't pay attention when she felt a presence behind her. A rag covered her mouth and an arm pulled her back into a hard body. She struggled for a few moments before blackness claimed her. Hours later, she woke to find herself contained in a coffin like space that was cold and clammy. The sound of an engine rumbled and the container she was in bounced. Wearing herself out by screaming and beating at her small prison, she lapsed into sleep waking every once in a while to scream for help. The next time she woke, she was in a dark room like area with another woman. It wasn't until days later that she was able to see where she was when he came and opened the door above.

Rico sat stunned at what Shawn had told her, she had been taken in broad daylight and no one saw anything.

"How long have I been missing, time down there didn't exist."

"A little over seven months, how did you get out of this place and do you have any idea where you were?"

"I used a bone from one of the bodies to dig a tunnel." She looked down at her scarred hands and showed them to Rico. "Kind of ruined me for those hand commercials I so wanted to do." She gave a little snort and broke down into tears. With her voice breaking, she told Rico that she walked for a long time through woods and fields until she collapsed. Rico wrapped her arms around her and rocked her; she could feel her anger boiling just below the surface but knew it would do neither of them any good. She needed to get a hold of a profiler and agents to go over the area near where Shawn had been found. If they could find where she was kept, they may be able to collect evidence, identify the remains, and solve some of the missing person cases. Wiping the tears from Shawn's face, she placed a kiss on her temple and hummed into her ear.

"Rico, Jeanne was a lesbian and I think he took me because of the T-shirt I had on."

"Why would you say that?"

"It said across the front 'Do I look straight to you?' And the more I think about it, I think he meant by impure wombs as women giving birth to homosexuals and by killing lesbians, he was riding the world of..."

"Ohh Gods Shawn..." She pulled back to look into worried green eyes.

"Does it bother you that I'm gay?" Her brows drew down over her nose when Rico busted out laughing. "Why are you laughing?"

"Because you happen to be sitting on the lap of the biggest dyke in the FBI."

"Guess it doesn't bother you then."

"No it doesn't. However, you just solved one part of what had my mind spinning. I have to call in a profiler and get him to work on this." She hugged Shawn tighter to her. "You want to call your mom?"

***

Shawn held the phone to her ear and wiped the tears from her face, glancing at Rico, she waited until the phone on the other end picked up. "Mom its Shawna…I'm OK." She waited for her mom to calm before she continued. "I was kidnapped, I'm in Virginia." She started sobbing uncontrollable so Rico took the

38

phone from her.   "Mrs. MacDonaill this is FBI Director Chamaune, Shawna is staying at my house with me."

"When can she come home, she needs to be here so I can take care of her."

"Ma'am at this point in time I feel that it would be both unsafe and unwise for her to be away from the protection of the FBI. Who ever kidnapped her is still out there."

"If he let her go, then why is it un-safe? I don't understand?"

"She wasn't released, she escaped. At this time her physical health is a concern."

"Why isn't she in a hospital?"

"That's something that..." Shawn took the phone from Rico. "I'll tell her." She caressed Rico's cheek and smiled. Rico sat and listened to the one sided conversation, and then drifted off into her own thoughts. She was quickly falling for the small woman and didn't know if that was a good thing at the time. After this was over, Shawn would return to her previous life and Rico would go back to being the hard ass FBI director. She stared off into the distance and was lost in the what if's when she felt Shawn press her face into the side of her neck.

"Are you OK?" She asked with a deep voice.

"She wanted to come here and take care of me, I told her that I was being taken care of and that I would call her every day."

"If you want, I could have her flown out here."

"Uhhmm no, she would have me so crazy that you would have to put me in the nut house."

"Are you sure?" Blue eyes connected with green and searched for an answer.

"Yeah, I'm happy here with you and mama." She wrapped her arms tighter around Rico and snuggled into her warmth.

"So this is where I'm lacking in the bedside manner thing?" Bridget was standing in the doorway with Bobby at her side.

Bobby grabbed her wives ear and gave it a yank. "If I ever catch you treating a patient like that...lets just say that you would need a doctor to put you back together."

Rico snorted at her friends bickering, she always found them amusing in there way of showing their love for each other.

"What brings you guys here?" She asked while noticing that Shawn was putting a strangle hold on her neck. "Shawn these are my friends Bobby and Bridget, they treated you at the hospital."

Frightened green eyes looked at the smiling women, sighing; she relaxed against Rico and held out her hand. "Sorry, I'm still jumpy around people. Thank you for helping me. I know I was a little freaked when I woke up."

"Yeah but Rico the tamer came to your rescue." Bobby hid behind her wife when Rico sent her "the look". "OK, so you came to our rescue."

"You are soo smooth baby." Bridget whispered. "Anyway, we brought some stuff for you to help put some weight back on." She held out a bag to Shawn and grinned at Rico.

Shawn opened the bag and pulled out a container of muscle builder and weight gain mix, six bottles of special vitamins and other items that would help in her recovery.

"Damn, with all that stuff and mama's cooking, you'll look like *Chyna* in a month." Rico looked at the huge container of muscle gain. "You guys wanna have supper with us, mama's cooking pot roast with all the trimmings."

"OK, but first we need to check on Shawn." Bridget wiggled her brows at Rico. "Make sure you're not laying down on the job."

***

Shawn was recovering faster than thought possible, Bridget was surprised to find the infections in her wounds gone and everything healing quickly and with little scarring. The scars on her back were a different story though; she would need plastic surgery to remove them. Bridget mentioned it to Shawn and gave her the name of the best plastic surgeon she knew. It would help with her emotional healing for the scars to be removed. However, Shawn thought little of it; she considered the scares a statement of her strength. She had survived what other's couldn't or didn't and each day when she looked at the faint scares, she would see the iron will that was hidden in her soul.

***

Mama handed Bobby a container with one of the blueberry cheesecakes she had baked earlier that day. Giving both women a tight hug and a kiss on their cheeks, she closed the door as they left. They were the only friends that Rico had and she always enjoyed it when they came to visit. Her daughter's sexual orientation had never been a problem for her; she just wished that she would find someone to share her life with. Rico had never had a relationship with anyone, always preferring to stay distanced from other women. So when she walked into the living room and found Shawn cuddled up close to Rico's side as she sat on the couch reading over a file, it brought a huge smile to her face. She leaned over the back of the couch and placed a kiss on both of there cheeks and told Rico that she would see them in the   morning.

Rico's eyes poured over the information in the file, she had contacted her assistant earlier that day and had him go back over the files on the missing women from her pet project. With the information she had given him, he was able to narrow the numbers down to women. Who were known lesbians, attended a college, and were of a European background. She figured that if this sick bastard thought he was Hitler, then he would be targeting European women to rid the world of their supposed perversions. He was going in a different direction than Hitler did and she was glad for it. The thought of someone copying the insane fuehrer, act for act was a little to much to for her to handle. The situation that was in front of her now was sickening enough. In the morning, she was to meet with other agents to walk the fields that surrounded where Shawn had been found. It may take days or weeks but deep in her gut, she knew that they would   find   where   she   was   kept   captive.

Closing the file, she placed it on the end table and then looked to see a sleeping Shawn. Her one small hand gripped Rico's shirttail, while the other twitched where it rested on her thigh. Leaning back a bit, she let her eyes trail across her features, noticing that the dark circles beneath her eyes had disappeared and some of the gauntness had filled in below her cheeks. She ran trembling fingers through her shaggy hair and sighed at how silky the strains felt. Green eyes opened to trap blue, Rico could then see that gold flecks danced in the background along with a low smoldering fire. Shawn moved so that her face Rico's large hand cupped her face. A small yawn forced its way from between pink lips.

Rico's voice was low; she brushed the backs of her fingers down Shawn's cheek. "Let's get you to bed."

"Are you coming?" She asked then blushed when she realized what she had just said. "I mean I sleep better when you're…"

"I'll be in later; I have some things to check on first."

"OK, goodnight then." She got up and leaned over to place a soft kiss on Rico's cheek, then went off to bed leaving a stunned FBI Director watching after her. Rico forgot all about the work that she was going to do, instead she sat and starred at the ceiling trying to figure out what just happened to her heart. She ran her fingers across where her cheek was still tingling and let it drift down to where her heart was pounding in her chest. "All that from a simple kiss on my cheek." She mumbled to herself and then slumped down on the couch, where she fell in to a dream filled sleep of sparkling green eyes watching over her.

***

Shawn stood bent over Rico; she placed her fingers to her neck and felt her pulse beating strong. Narrowing her eyes, she looked into the slit blue eyes and felt a shiver race down her back. Rico was sound asleep but her eyes were open. She had never seen anything so freaky in her life.

"Rico you're scaring the hell outta me here." She lifted one eyelid up and jumped when the other opened and looked at her. "Do you always sleep with your eyes open?"

Rico was confused, she blinked her eyes a few times and yawned. "Huh?"

"Never mind, come to bed." Shawn took her by her hand and pulled her up from the couch, she never let her go until they were in the bedroom. She pushed her down onto the edge of the bed and pulled her t-shirt up over her head. Her face blushed when she saw that Rico wore nothing but the T-shirt. Pushing her back on the bed, she removed her shoes and socks and then pointed to her Levi's. "Off." Sleepy blue eyes looked at her and then down at her Levi's. She didn't move a muscle, her arms stayed at her sides and a light snore came from her. "Unbelievable." Shawn mumbled before unfastening her Levi's and pulling them off. "No underwear either, who would have guessed that the FBI Director preferred to go native?" She couldn't help but let her eyes wonder over the muscular body of her friend. The heat in her face was enough to cause sweat to form on her upper lip. Closing her eyes, she swung Rico's legs onto the bed and pulled the blankets over her. When she got into bed, she felt a warm body spoon against her back and hot breath caress the back of her neck. Trembles ran through her body when a hand nestled between her breasts. Taking a calming breath, she closed her eyes and let the closeness of Rico's body lull her into sleep.

***

A blurry blue eye popped open when the erotic dream she was having turned out not being a dream at all. A warm body was pressed up close to her back, moist lips kissed and then a hot tongue licked the nape of her neck. A small hand brushed through the short-cropped curls at her apex and slipped between her swollen lips to find the wetness flowing from within. Her hips thrust forward on their own accord, panic took over and she grabbed the small hand and removed it from between her thighs. Moving Shawn's hand to her own thigh, Rico looked over her shoulder to see her sound asleep. "Why couldn't you be a sleep walker?" She mumbled under her breath. The throbbing and fullness between her legs called for her attention, she tried to ignore her body but lost the fight when Shawn's hand started to wonder again. Sitting up, she sat on the edge of the bed and jumped when a small hand caressed her ass. A low rumbling bounced around in her chest as she stumbled on weak knees to the bathroom. Turning on the shower, she adjusted it to where it was cold but not heart stopping, she all ready had a heart stopper in   her   bed.

Shawn rolled over and leaned off the side of the bed, a huge grin formed on her face as she heard Rico let out a yelp. "That's for scaring me last night with the eyeball thing." She brought her fingers up to her nose and breathed in Rico's scent. "Better leave some cold water." She mumbled then pulled Rico's pillow   to   her   chest.

The water cascaded down over Rico's shivering back, giving up on the cold shower; she adjusted it to her normal temperature. Running a hand down her stomach to her throbbing center, she couldn't hold back the whimpers when her hips started thrusting forward. Bracing one hand on the shower wall, she stroked her engorged clit, her legs started to shake with the onslaught of her climax. Moving her fingers faster, a deep moan burst from her lips with her release. Leaning forward, she rested her head on the cool tiles and waited for her legs to stop shaking.

Shawn lay on her side listening to Rico in the shower, her own body throbbing and on edge. Clutching Rico's pillow tighter to her chest, she closed her eyes. The second she heard the deep moan echo in the shower, her hips jerked forward with her climax. She had never had an orgasm without being touched before. If Rico touched her, she would probably pass out. Tremors still traveled through her body minutes later when Rico came into the room wrapped in a towel. Feigning sleep, she stayed still and watched thru one slit eye as Rico pulled on a pair of running shorts, sports bra and her tennis shoes and left the room. When it was safe to move, she climbed out of bed, cleaned up in the bathroom, went into the kitchen, and found Marie drinking coffee at the table. Her face turned a deep red, she was ready to turn and run back to the bedroom when Marie spoke to her.

"Mornin wee bit, have some coffee." She looked up and grinned at her. "Whatcha do ta Rico, she ran out of here dragging poor Jed with her, mumbling something about running the Boston marathon."

Shawn got a cup from the cabinet and slouched down into a chair; keeping her eyes glued to her cup, she shrugged her shoulders.

"Uhh huh…did something devious did cha." She started chuckling.

"I paid her back for scaring me last night; she fell asleep on the couch with her…"

"Eyes open? Scary damn thing, her papa used ta do it to." She leaned forward and wiggled her eyebrows. "So…"

"I can't tell you." She said in a low voice.

"Ya teased her did ya?" She burst out laughing and it grew worse when Shawn turned bright red and slipped further down into her chair.

"How did you know?"

Wiping tears from her eyes, Marie took a deep calming breath. "She runs when she's sexually frustrated. My wee one could out run all the marathoners. I'm talking years of frustration!"

"You talk about things like that with her?"

"Of course, don't all mama's and daughters?"

"If I mention sex around my mom, she changes the subject." She looked at Marie with a cocked eyebrow. "So there's no…significant other that's going to come and kick my ass?"

"Wee one has never dated so you're safe."

"Oohh boy." She covered her face and groaned. *She's probably a virgin on top of it.* She thought to herself.

"Get dressed and ya can help me in the garden. That way when wee one gets back, I won't have ta do CPR on one of ya from embarrassment."

***

Rico sprinted off into the field behind her mama's house with Jed running behind her. She kept looking back over her shoulder at the little goat trying to keep up with her. She loved the little pest but times like these she missed having a dog. Slowing her pace, she let Jed catch up to her. She let her get within a few steps, bent over and head butted with her then jogged a few paces away. They continued to play like that until Rico's forehead began to get sore.

"Come on Jed, let's go get some breakfast." Grabbing Jed's tail, she laughed when she tucked her rear and let out a long yell of Maaa. "Wimp!" She didn't know that the entire time she had been playing with Jed that she had an audience watching from the garden. When she jogged past, she heard her mama yell to her.

"Put some ice on your head, people think I beat ya or somethin."

***

Rico jumped in the shower and couldn't help but think of what she had done in there a short time before. Groaning over her lack of strength, she washed her hair and lathered her body. Taking her mind off her body, she thought of ways to search the area where Shawn had been found, thinking of grids and number of manpower she would have for that morning had her mind occupied. The more she thought of what she had to do the madder she got, her eyes changed to an icy color, a stoic mask dropped over her features as she climbed from the shower. Pulling her black fatigue pants, black FBI t-shirt and black jungle boots from her closet, she dressed hurriedly. Going into her office, she unfolded all the maps she had and picked the best one. She wanted to be able to show the agents exactly where to start and give them an idea of the obstacles they would encounter. The ringing of her cell phone sent curses flowing from her lips, flipping it open she barked into it.

"What?"

"Good morning to you to Chamaune, are you going to help us this morning or are all the agents and sheriff's deputy's going to play ring around the rosy in that damn field?"

"What's the matter Stan afraid some wild animal will run in front of you and you'll be without a BBQ grill to cook it?"

"Haaa! No sleep last night Rico, you have to calm down that social life of yours. Ohh I forgot you don't have one of those!" He chuckled because he knew she would have a look on her face that could crack a mirror from 40 paces off. "Anyway, I managed to round up some extra bodies; we'll have the volunteer firefighters and the regular guys for a few hours before they get off   duty."

A wicked grin came to her face; she knew that she could count   on   her   assistant   to   wrangle   extra   help.

"I'll be there in ten or fifteen minutes, get everyone lined up and as soon as I get there we'll start walking." She closed her phone and hung it off her webbed belt. Taking her shoulder holsters from the coat rack near the door, she swung it across her back and fastened the extra leather strap that she had sewn on under her breasts. Running her hands through her still damp hair, she took a deep breath and prepared herself to face Shawn and her   mama.

***

"The mighty warrior off ta slay monsters." Marie replied as she tossed her daughter a bottle of water. "Ya better take some trail bars with ya, if I know ya; you'll starve ta death out there before   ya   think   of   food."
A dark brow arched over an ice blue eye, shaking her head she grabbed a few trail bars from the pantry, showed them to her mama and dropped them into her cargo pocket. "Water and food I'm set, I don't know how long I'll be out there so..."

Getting up from the table, she winked at Shawn and pulled Rico into a tight hug."Don't worry wee one, we'll hold down the fort and yes I'll set the alarm, secure the hatches and force   feed   Shawn."

"Thanks mama." She whispered and then headed out the side door. With one glance over her shoulder into green eyes, she gave her a stoic look and then left.   Heaviness fell onto Shawn's heart, it hurt that Rico had not said one word to her that morning and just left for who only knows how long. Her eyes became misty as she heard the sound of the Blazer pulling away from the cabin.

"Mama   is   she   mad   at   me   this   morning?"

"Wee bit, ya have ta understand, that Jericho has no idea how to express herself when it comes ta other people. She's so good at her job 'cuz she can distance herself from the horrors of

47

the world. If ya were ta see her in her office, ya would run ta the door without looking back."

"I can't help but think that I caused her stoic mood today, I shouldn't have teased her like I did." She wiped the tears from her eyes and looked worriedly at Marie. "Is there anything I can do?"

Marie pulled the small woman into her arms and held her as she cried. "Don't worry about Rico, she'll come around as soon as she scares the hell outta all the agents today."

***

Rico searched the passenger seat for her map, her temper exploded when she remembered that she had left it at home on her desk. Slapping her hand on the steering wheel, she yelped when a bruise formed on the palm of her hand. "I can't believe I forgot the fucking map!" She yelled at the car that blew past her. "Slow the fuck down you asshole, before you cause an accident!" Slapping the flashing light onto the dashboard, she terrorized other drivers into slowing down. Taking the side road off Rt. 9, she drove taking the dangerous curves like a road raged maniac.

***

A loud thump hit the ground as the concrete slab fell over the pit shutting off the screams coming from below. After hours of cruising near the college, the Fuehrer had found another victim to add to his collection. The young woman had been jogging alone early that morning on one of the gravel roads just outside of Shepherdstown. He normally went out of state for his victims but with the escape of the last one, his hunger uncontrollable and lack of time, he settled for an area native. He wasn't worried about the police investigating anything; he had been checking the newspapers and no body had been found. He called the hospital, pretended to be a worried family member and needed to know if his sister had been admitted. When they told him that no young females in their twenties had been admitted he knew that he was safe. With a self-satisfied smirk on his face, he clicked his heels together, crossed his hands behind his back and stared off into the distance for a few moments before getting into his truck and driving away. At the top of his lungs, he sang the German anthem and tore down the center of the road.

**

Rico went around a hairpin turn hugging the edge of the road; she yanked the wheel to the right to avoid the on coming half ton truck. The passenger side wheels dropped off into the ditch, the force threw her up against the steering wheel and into the rear view mirror. The Blazer shuddered to a stop after spinning back towards the road, the rear wheels were stuck down into the knee-deep ditch filled with water and mud. Leaning back into the seat, Rico took a ragged breath and felt a sharp pain in her chest. Waiting until the pain left her; she got out of her Blazer and cussed a blue streak. She didn't know if putting it in four wheel drive would get her out, she was only about three miles from where Stan was waiting, so if it came down to it she could have one of the sheriffs pull her out. Wiping what she thought was sweat from her forehead; she brought her hand away covered with   blood.
"Fucking great, God damn fucking asshole drivers!" She kicked the tire of the Blazer and jumped back when it slid further into the ditch. Throwing her hands in the air, she screamed. "Sonofabitch!" Taking her chances, she got in, dropped it into four-wheel drive and floored the gas pedal. A loud screeching came from the front tires as they tried to grip the road. Rocking it back and forth, she finally got the Blazer's wheels to grip and with a tear of metal, it made it back onto the road. Pulling up the road a bit and away from the dangerous curve, she got out and shoved up her catalytic converter, exhaust pipe, and muffler to the edge of the road. She would have to remember to pick them up later. Taking a quick look underneath, she saw a few drops of oil hit the ground. Now she was pissed enough to start doing drive by shootings. Pulling a bandana from her cargo pocket and looking at her reflection in the side view mirror, she wiped at the stinging area above her right eyebrow. Blood was streaming from

the four-inch gash that the rear view mirror had done. Taking on a thick Irish brogue, she berated herself. "Wee one, that's what the seatbelts are fer! Use 'em next time!" Folding the bandana, she wrapped it around her head, got back in her Blazer and took off towards where she was supposed to be. If anyone had been in the Blazer during this short trek, they would have been deaf from all the screaming and yelling she was doing. However, nothing could compare to the loud noise the engine was making without its exhaust system. Seeing the collection of vehicles up ahead, she pulled off into the parking lot for the flea market and got out with a bit of dizziness. Shaking it off, she went in search of her assistant Stan.

***

"Where the Hell have you been?" He asked her as she came up to stand beside him. "Jesus Rico, what happened to you?" He reached out to touch her forehead and yanked back his hand   when   she   growled   at   him.

"Mother fucker ran me off the road." She wiped the seeping blood that trailed down her temple. "I tore the shit out of my   Blazer."

"Rico, why don't you just go home, we can handle this out here." He realized his mistake when she grabbed him by his jacket and lifted him off his feet. Silvery blue eyes drilled into as a deep growling voice came from between snarling lips. "I want this sick fuck! You have no idea what he did to Shawna!" She lowered him to the ground but kept a hold of him. "She looks like a concentration camp prisoner, he branded her with the swastika and cut S's in her back." Going nose to nose with him, she jabbed him in his chest with her index finger. "I want this fucker!"

Adjusting his jacket, he turned and barked out orders for everyone to line up and start walking. "I don't care if you find bear shit, I want it bagged and tagged you hear me!" He turned slowly when he felt a hand on his shoulder seeing Rico he flinched.

"Sorry   Stan,   it's   been   a   bad   morning."

"Is Shawna doing OK, I mean for her to escape and wander around out here for who knows how long in the condition

50

that   you   described."
"One   word   Stan,   Mama."
He gave her a grin; he knew how Marie acted with anyone sick or having any kind of problem. "OK, so she's being spoiled   rotten."

***

Marie mixed another glass of goat's milk and the chocolate weight gainer that Bridget had brought beside Shawna where she was doing some research on the internet. She had asked earlier if Marie thought Rico would mind if she used her computer. Marie waved a hand at her and told her "the Hell with my crabby kid, use what ever ya wants." So now, she was surfing and trying to find anything she could on Hitler, the Third Reich and SS Troopers. She starred at a web page that showed a big black and white swastika on a red background. Drawing the image on a note pad, she rearranged the legs and came up with the Star of David. It was like a hidden message, the most known and feared symbol in Europe during the 40's was the broken down sign of the chosen people. Not only did he break the people,   he   broke   their   symbol.
"Have ya found anything ta help Wee one?"
"Not really Mama, there's a lot of stuff here that explains about the Elite Troopers and other things. I haven't any idea what I'm looking for." She looked over her shoulder into blue eyes so much   like   Rico's.

"Well, why dontcha take a break, supper's ready. I hope ya like roasted chicken." She squeezed her shoulder lightly. "I'll have ya fit in no time, made sour dough rolls and I have fresh butter   ta   go   with   them."
In the short time she had been at Rico's, she had begun to feel better and could tell that her body was starting to fill out a little. She could eat more at one sitting without feeling sick. Then with the vitamins and protein drinks, she had more energy. Running her fingers through her hair, she sighed. "Could you cut my hair for me? It's all shaggy and I feel like a bum."

"After supper and your shower, I'll get out my scissors. Now come on wee bit, foods getting cold."

***

Rico's head was pounding, her shirt was soaked with sweat and she had mud, briars and leaves in places that they shouldn't be. While walking in the field, she had been the only one to find a sinkhole that was hidden by tall weeds. After falling a good ten foot down and landing in muck, she looked up to have the loose dirt above fall down on her head. Now feeling like the bottom of a skid row bums shoe, to make matters worse it was getting dark and starting to rain. Stopping in her tracks, she looked back in the distance but couldn't see any of their vehicles. "All right people, lets go home!" She yelled out across the field to the others. "We'll try again tomorrow, be here at 7am." She waved over her shoulder and took off at a jog towards where the road was and then to the flea market parking lot. Pulling her filthy t-shirt off, she tossed it into the back, crawled behind the wheel and sighed. Her entire body was starting to stiffen up. She wanted nothing more than to get home, take a nice long hot bath and go to bed. Then green eyes invaded her thoughts. "Don't even go there Rico, you're supposed to be protecting her." A loud bark of laughter burst forth. "Hell, I need protection from her!" Minutes later Rico pulled up to her garage, her head was pounding like a bass drum from all the noise her Blazer had been making. Slamming the door, she limped towards the kitchen door. After hitting the alarm off, she stepped into the small mudroom and shed her clothes. Dropping them into a pile, she walked naked towards her bathroom under the scrutiny of stunned green eyes. Shawn waited an hour after hearing the bathtub being filled, getting up from where she had been watching the news, she shut off the TV and went into Rico's bedroom. As she passed the bathroom, she looked in to see Rico asleep in the tub. Walking slowly towards her, she reached out, touched her shoulder and then felt a tight grip on her wrist. She yelped   and   tried   to   pull   away.
"Rico it's me, let go." Blue eyes opened, and a large hand

immediately released Shawn's wrist.

"Sorry, I do that out of reflex." A low groan came to her lips when she tried to get out of the tub. She looked when Shawn gasped and reached out a hand to touch her temple.

"You're hurt, what happened?"

"I had a fight with a ditch, rearview mirror, steering wheel and a sinkhole."

"I'm glad you didn't run into any bad guys." She deadpanned. "Let me help you."

"I'm all right, just a little sore." She placed a hand on either side of the tub and tried to push herself up. "On second thought, I could use some help."

***

Rico sat leaning against the headboard with Shawn sitting on the edge of the bed at her side. She had fought for all of two seconds against Shawn putting butterfly strips on the gash above her eyebrow. Shawn threatened to go and get mama and have her fix her up. Now with seven strips holding the gash closed and four aspirins, she was suffering small fingers checking her ribs and chest. She could see the deep bruise above her right breast that ran to the center of her chest.

"OK, scoot down in the bed and get some sleep and I'll see you in the morning." Rico gave her a questioning look when Shawn moved towards the door and turned the light off. "Where you going?"

Shawn dropped her head and sniffed back the sudden tears.

"I'll be in the living room." She turned when she felt a warm hand on her upper arm.

"Come to bed Shawn." Rico pulled her towards the bed; she slipped under the covers and moved over giving Shawn room to lie down. "Come on lay down and get some sleep." Shawn lay down and turned to face away from Rico, she stared across the now dark room. Rico moved closer to her back, taking a slow breath, she spooned up against the small body and placed her hand across her hollow stomach. She heard the sniffing and buried her face in the soft hair at the base of Shawn's neck. "It's OK, I'm here go to sleep."

***

A cold chill blew across Shawn's bare legs; the blankets lay unused beside her where she had kicked them off. Grumbling and trying to find the warmth of Rico's body came up disappointing empty. A green eye cracked open and searched the side of the bed that should have held the tall Director, instead was a forgotten FBI t-shirt. Pulling the shirt to her nose, she took in the soft scent of her friend. It gave her a sense of something exotic and comforting. She would ask mama what cologne Rico wore because her mind just wasn't up to trying to figure the scent out. Pulling the covers back over her body, she snuggled down into Rico's pillow with the shirt clutched to her chest and fell asleep. Rico scrounged in the refrigerator for something to eat before she went back out to the fields to search for what she hoped for was not another encounter with a sinkhole. Her back stiffened at the sound of a growl behind her, putting the piece of chicken back in the dish, she jumped when a small foot connected with her ass.

"Get out of there and sit down, ya nots eaten chicken fer breakfast." Mama pointed a finger at her and then to a chair. "Sit or I'll kick ya again." She smiled at the defeated look on her tall child's face. She enjoyed terrorizing her; it was a mother's right as far as she was concerned. "Where's wee bit?" Her voice low and not amused one bit at being caught doing something her mother wouldn't stand for as to not having a proper breakfast. She mumbled.
"Sleeping."

"Haul yer ass in there and wake her up, and ya be nice ta her." She turned to hold Rico in her frozen state of being half way out of her chair. "Ya have no idea how ya hurt her yesterday. She cried half the morning in my arms. Should be ashamed of yerself ya should."

"How did I hurt her?" Rico was confused; she couldn't remember anything that she had done to Shawn.

54

"Open up yer eyes knot head, ya ignored her like she was the bloody plague."

"But mama she...well I..."

"I knows all abouts what she did ta ya." She chuckled at the deep color Rico's face turned. "It was revenge fer scaring her ta death."

"She told cha, how did I do that?" Rico started pacing behind her chair, running a hand through her hair she stopped to stare at her mama. "All right nows, ya gonna let me suffer here aren't cha?" She slapped her forehead and then let out a deep groan from the sharp pain in her head. "Gods, how come I always end up with your accent when I get my..."

"Dander up, cuz ya forgets that ya wasn't born here. Anyways, yeah she told me and it was fer sleeping with yer eyes open. She thought ya was dead."

"I do not sleep with my eyes...shit." She dropped down in the chair, dropped her head down onto crossed arms, and let out another groan of pain.

"Been meanin ta ask ya, who clobbered ya in yer noggin?" She told her mama about the accident the day before and that she would have to fix her Blazer before she would be able to drive it. In addition, about how she had fallen into a sink hole and banged up her knee and twisted her ankle. Determined not to loose the battle of having to stay home, she said that she wouldn't stay out as long today because she had some stuff to look up on the FBI's data base. After her mama had nodded her head in defeat, she told her to go wake up Shawn for breakfast. She walked slowly into the room and sat on the edge of the bed, she didn't want to face the fact that Shawn had managed to arouse her body to such a fevered pitch so quickly. She never thought of sex as being a part of life, it had never had a place in hers and what Shawn had done in her eyes was weaken her to primal feelings. She attentively ran fingers through dark blonde hair and sighed at the silky touch. She knew that Shawn was wiggling her way through the walls she built around her heart. Chipping away at them a little bit each day until they would eventually fall in to a crumbling mass. A soft sigh came from between moist parted lips and then a small hand came from under the covers clutching her old t-shirt. Rico smiled as she watched Shawn bring it up to her nose, take a deep breath and snuggle further into her pillow. Rico hated to wake her from her deep sleep but she knew if she didn't then mama would kick her ass literally. Leaning close to a small ear, she whispered. That it was time to wake up and breakfast was ready. Pulling back a little, she saw a green eye open a ways and then a light blush cover Shawn's face when she realized that she had Rico's t-shirt up to her nose.

"You can have the shirt, it's an old one." With one last caress to a pink cheek, Rico went back out to the kitchen with a goofy grin on her face.

"Is she up?" Mama asked then raised an eyebrow at the look on Rico's face. "What's the look for?" Rico's face blushed as she looked down at the floor.

"It's nothing really but you'll see soon enough."

"Ya didn't give her a love bit or somethin did ya?"

"Mama! Geez, sometimes I just don't know about you." She took her seat and waited for mama to put a plate of scrambled eggs, bacon and toast in front of her. She looked up when she heard a loud yawn to see Shawn dressed in the old t-shirt taking the chair next to her. She couldn't help but reach out and run her fingers through the tousled hair.

"Your hair's shorter."

"Yeah, I had mama cut it." She looked shyly at Rico. "Does it look OK...not saying that mama isn't good but...?"

"Yes it looks very nice." She brushed the bangs back from her forehead. "It suits you." Giving her a lopsided smile, she turned back to her plate and all most choked when mama placed a heaping plate in front of Shawn. "Mama, that's enough for a small army."

"Yep, and that's exactly what she eats like." Mama looked at the shirtsleeves hanging past Shawn's elbows and snorted. "She stole your shirt huh?"

"Nope, gave it to her."

"Gotta mark this on the calendar, wee one gave her favorite shirt away." Rico glanced out of the corner of her eye to see Shawn's gaping mouth.

"She can have anything she wants." She traded a grin with Shawn and went back to eating.

***

After she was finished eating, Rico placed a kiss on Shawn's temple, kissed her mama's cheek and headed out the door leaving a blushing Shawn staring at the door. "Mama what did you say to her?" Blue eyes twinkled back at her; mama shrugged her shoulders and snorted at the raised eyebrow look. "Kicked her in the ass this mornin s'all." Shawn went to the kitchen window when she heard a loud rumbling coming from the garage and then saw Rico leave on her motorcycle.

She turned with surprised eyes to mama. "She has a motorcycle?"

"Yep, Blazer's tore up." She placed the dirty dishes in the dishwasher and turned it on. "She says it needs fixed before she can   drive   it."

"Would   she   get   mad   if   I   looked ·   at   it?"

"Nah, go ahead and have a look. If ya need anything I'll be at home."

***

Shawn was lying up under the Blazer with a torque wrench she had found in Rico's toolbox, she was on the last bolt on the oil pan. She had found an extra gasket for it hanging on the wall and decided to just change it instead of taking a chance and having it leak after the bolts were re-torqued. She had made a list of the parts Rico would need to get it back on the road, if she picked them up, she would put them on for her. Fixing cars was something that she had done to earn extra money at college. After reading all the manuals she could get her hands on, she became the parking lot mechanic for all the women and some of the useless men. Crawling out from under the Blazer, she walked towards Mama's house. It would be the first time she was in the older women's house, she almost forgot that she had one since she was always in Rico's. Knocking on the screen door at the

57

front of the house, she could smell a cinnamon scent wafting in the air. Her stomach let out a loud roar and reminded her that she hadn't eaten anything since breakfast. "Ya don't hafta knock wee bit, just come on in." She waved Shawn into her immaculate house and headed towards her kitchen. "I'm making apple dumplings   for   us."

"I fixed the oil pan on the Blazer and I made a list of parts that Rico will need to get it back on the road. If she picks them up,   I'll   put   them   on   for   her."

"Another grease monkey aye? I'll take ya ta gets the parts, I have her checkbook." Mama wiggled her eyebrows at her. "We can   go   into   town   right   now   if   ya   want?"

"OK, then I can get it finished so she can drive it tomorrow." She sat down in a kitchen chair and looked at her greasy hands. "Can I ask you something about Rico?" Mama turned from what she was doing and nodded her head. "Her clothes all have this spicy type scent to them, what is it?" Mama chuckled at the blush running up Shawn's face.

"It's sandalwood oil, she uses it in the shower. She brought a lot of   it   back   from   when   she   was   in   India." Green eyes widened. "She's been to India? I've only been to Shannon Ireland, I went to visit family one year." Blue eyes widened at the mention of Shannon Ireland, she walked closer to Shawna and spoke in her native language and was surprised when Shawn   answered   her   back.

"We're from Shannon, it's been years since we've been back   home."

"You mean Rico was born in Ireland?" She asked with surprise   in   her   voice.

"And raised, came here ta get away from all the bullshit going   on   over   there."

"But   she   doesn't   have   an   accent."

"Ohh yes she does, get her flustered and she sounds like me." She winked at her. "Worse though, she stutters."

***

58

Rico unrolled the map that she had remembered to take from her office, inside was a note written in elegant script.

Rico

I hope you don't mind, I graphed out the map for you into sections to make it easier. I remember hearing water while I was walking,   I   hope   that   helps   a   little.

Love

Shawn

A smile came to Rico's face; Shawn had no idea how much help she had done, with not only the map but the river. The river only ran on one side of Rt. 340 where you could possible hear it. That was the road that came off Rt. 9 and the same road that she took to get to where she had been meeting the others. It cut down on the amount of land that they would have to search. After assigning two people a grid to search, she took one to do by herself. She always worked alone because she didn't trust anyone to not get in her way. She figured that they were searching at least three miles of ground a day and that it would take at least two weeks doing it on foot at the rate they were going. She would make some calls in the morning to see about getting one of the FBI's choppers with the heat sensor in it. It may help to determine if there is a temperature difference somewhere out there, that's abnormal. She had tried to get tracking dogs but they were all in different locations working on a number of things that were deemed more important. They had been out there searching for six hours and her knee and ankle were throbbing with each beat of her heart. She called for them to stop and mark where they were and that they would try again in the morning. Walking up to Stan, she pulled him aside and told him that he would be in charge the next morning because she had to go into the office to pick up some reports and to search the database for more information.

"Rico, if I'm not mistaking you're on vacation. Why don't you   let   me   handle   the   office   stuff?"

"I appreciate the offer Stan, but I have to stop by the

Chevy dealership and get the parts for my Blazer. Plus you know me, I like doing the research stuff."

***

Shawn lowered the Blazer down from the floor-jack; she had put a complete exhaust system on from the manifolds all the way to the tailpipe. Now exhausted and wanting nothing more than to take a nice hot bath and relax until Rico got home. She missed her when she wasn't around, she knew that she was trying to find the asshole who, had kidnapped her and killed all the others but she wished that she had more time with her. Rico was really the first friend she had; the people that she went to college with were just mere acquaintances. Not to mention that just seeing Rico made her pulse race and her mouth go dry. After her bath, Shawn went into Rico's office and booted up her PC. Going onto the web, she found a site that had all the concentration camps on it that the SS Troops were in charge of. She double clicked on a picture of the camp Gorlitz and felt her heart stop in her chest. There were pictures of prisoners standing outside of a high fence topped with serpentine wire. Tears formed in her eyes from seeing the shape the men were in, she pulled up her t-shirt, looked at her bony hips, and sunk in stomach. Racking sobs overcame her; she was seeing herself on the screen. She now knew why Rico didn't want anything to do with her on a more emotional level. She looked half-dead. Rico was standing in the living room when she heard the sobbing coming from her office. Moving slowly down the hall she stopped outside the door and saw Shawn slumped over in the chair crying. Moving closer, she saw the picture on the screen and held back a sigh. She knew what had upset her small friend, but she didn't know what to do about it. Taking a deep breathe, she moved to stand beside the chair and then kneeled down.
"Shawn?" She spoke in a whisper.
She lifted her tear stained face to look at Rico and then cried out. "I'm…just…like them." Rico pulled her into her arms and held her tight, rocking her in her arms, she whispered calming words into her ear. "No one will ever want me now." She

sobbed   into   Rico's   chest.
    "That's   not   true   Shawn."
    She pulled back and looked into kind blue eyes. "Yeah right, look at me." She pulled up her T-shirt and showed her ribcage.   "I'm   nothing   but   skin   and   bones."
    "Shawn, now listen to me." She cupped her face between her hands. "It takes time but you'll put all your weight back on." She placed a kiss on her forehead and pulled her back against her chest. "It's what's on the inside that counts, not the outside. You look just fine to me, so stop worrying about it OK?" She took a small hand and kissed her knuckles then saw all the grease stains on her hands and arms. "Why are your hands so dirty?" A muffled voice came from against her chest. She leaned back and looked into downcast eyes. "You fixed my Blazer?"
    "Mama took me to get the parts; I put it all back together while you were gone." She looked up into a beaming smile. "I like working on cars." She shrugged her shoulders and blushed. Rico leaned in and place a soft kiss on her lips, then pulled her back against her chest.
"Thank   you."
    Shawn's lips tingled from the soft kiss, her heart raced in her chest so fast that she was afraid that Rico would be able to feel it. She had never expected her to kiss her for fixing her Blazer but it was most welcome. Snuggling deeper into Rico's chest, she sniffed back her tears and took comfort in the warm arms, scent of sandalwood and what was Rico's own scent.
    "Have   you   eaten   yet   Shawn?"
    "Earlier,   but   I'm   hungry."
    "Let's   go   see   what   mama   left   for   us."
    With plates piled high with BBQ ribs, they sat side by side on the couch, watched TV, and shared a gallon of milk that they drank from the jug. Rico knew that if her mama saw them drinking from the jug, they would both be getting a kick to their asses. After the ribs were gone, Shawn brought out a bowl of apple dumplings with ice cream on top of them and two spoons. By the time they had finished all the food, both women's eyes were drooping closed. Lying side by side on the couch, they drifted off to sleep.

***

Shawn was the first one to wake that morning, she listened to the steady thump below her ear and felt the rise and fall of Rico's chest. Snuggling deeper in to the soft breasts beneath her face, she knew this was where she wanted to be every morning. Wrapping long silky hair around her fingers, she drifted back to sleep. Rico stirred from sleep when she felt fingers brushing her neck; tilting her head to the side, she saw small fingers twisting a strand of her hair around a thumb and index finger. Brushing back Shawn's hair from her face, she saw that she was still sleeping and drooling on her chest. For some reason it didn't bother her, any one else and she would have dumped them on the floor. Placing a kiss on the crown of her head, she eased out from under her and headed for the bathroom to take a shower. She had fallen asleep the night before still dirty from walking the fields; she hoped that she didn't have any ticks burrowing into her skin somewhere or that they had found a new home on Shawn. That would earn her a swift kick in the ass from mama. Adjusting the water, she shed her clothes and climbed under the hot water. Dropping her head forward, she let the pounding force of the water ease the stiff muscles of her neck and shoulder. She stood there for long moments thinking of the last time she stood like this in the shower. A fire started at her beating heart and shot down to swirl at her center, she imagined small fingers caressing her aching body and bringing it to the edge of euphoric heights and then tossing it over into the abyss. Her mind ran away on her, leaving her with nothing but her throbbing center and aching nipples that begged to be touched. One hand rose to cup a breast as the other traveled south to ease the pressure that was built there. That was until she heard her name called and looked to see Shawn's shadow on the other side of the shower   door.

"Rico,   step   back!"

"Huh? Why?" Just then, the toilet flushed and steaming hot water missed her by scant inches. "Hey! Ya could have warned me!" The shower door opened and Shawn with glinting

62

eyes and a crooked grin pointed a finger at Rico's chest.

"I told you to step back, what did you think I was talking about?" She wiggled an eyebrow and snorted when Rico's mouth worked a few times but no words came forth.

"I thought...you..." Her face turned a deep red color and it wasn't from the heat of the water. Shawn picked up what she was thinking by the color of her face and the trembling of her hands.

"Later hot stuff." She smacked her on her ass, turned the hot water off and ran from the bathroom listening as Rico let out a bellow that had the walls vibrating. Pulling one of Rico's t-shirts from her dresser, she changed out of the clothes she had slept in and pulled the large t-shirt on and a pair of sweatpants. She was going to start trying to work on gaining some muscle back by lifting the small dumbbells she had found lying in Rico's office. They were only small five-pound weights but in her present condition, they were more than enough of a challenge for her. Curling them upward, she walked out to the kitchen to start a pot of coffee for when Rico was finished with her shower. She wondered if maybe she should hide under the sink from her, after trying to turn her into an icicle in the shower. Getting out the frying pan and eggs, she started to make them breakfast when mama and Jed came through the side door into the kitchen.

"Go gets the wee one Jed." Mama told the little goat who then took off yelling 'maaa' at the top of her lungs. "You're up kinda late aren't cha wee bit?"

"Ohh well we were up kinda late last night."

"Uhh huh...and what were ya two doin?"

"Raiding the refrigerator." She gave her a crooked grin. They both turned when they heard Rico yell and then the sound of little hooves coming towards them. In seconds, Jed came into the kitchen with a towel hanging from her mouth.

"Rotten little goat!" Rico barked when she came into the kitchen dressed in a dark suit and looking like Agent Dana Scully. Shawn's mouth dropped open and hit her chest, her mouth went dry and she heard whistles in her ears when all the blood from her brain rushed south.

"Gods help me." She mumbled and then grabbed on to the

edge of the counter to stop from falling over. Wiping the sweat that had formed on her upper lip, she let her eyes hungrily travel the tall body before her until she locked eyes with pale amused blue eyes. Rico gave her a raised eyebrow and a small smirk.

"What?" she asked as she looked back and forth between Shawn and her mama.

"I swear Rico ya needs ta look in a mirror sometime, block headed..." The rest went unheard because mama lowered her voice to not embarrass her daughter.

Shawn found words rushing from her mouth and didn't realize what she was saying until it was to late. "You're the most striking woman I've ever seen." She dropped her head shyly and looked at her bare feet.

"I'm nothing special, just an old FBI Director." She gave her mama a snarl when she heard her snort and saw her roll her blue eyes.

"Right wee one, that's why every male and female falls on the floor when ya walks past 'em."

"I scare them, they drop from fright."

"Uhhh huh, now sits down, wee bits making breakfast as soon as she gets outta her stupor."

Rico walked over to her and lifted her chin with two fingers. "Do you want to come with me, I'm going to my office and you might be able to help with some information?"

"But I'm not dressed for...I've never been..."

Rico gave her a lopsided smile and kissed her forehead."Put some Levi's on and some shoes, that's good enough for me."

After breakfast, they headed into Tyson's corner to where the FBI's building was. Shawn took in all the sights that they passed on the way, she was amazed at all the buildings and shopping centers that littered the hour drive. What had her nerves on end was the traffic; she was used to the slow moving life of Texas. This was like the Indianapolis speedway, cars flew past them going at least 80mph. She didn't know if she would be able to handle driving in a city like this. She starred wide eyed out the window.

"None of these people have any sense when it comes to driving." Rico said as she jumped out the lane she was in to avoid a car that crossed over and cut her off. "This is one of the reasons I live so far away from work, I hate the city and anything to do with it." Shawn turned in the seat to look at her companion's profile. "I wouldn't be able to live in this type of place, to much noise and mass confusion. I like it nice and quiet, where you can sit outside and hear the birds and crickets." Whipping into the far right lane, she hit the gas pedal and grinned at the pick-up her Blazer now had. "You tuned this thing up didn't you?"

"Well yeah a little. When I changed the spark plugs I noticed that it wasn't firing quite right, so I timed it." She blushed shyly when Rico glanced over at her.
"But I don't have a timing light."
"I did it by ear, I have really good hearing and you know for some reason, I can see in the dark." She scrunched up her face and look at Rico. "I think it's from being in that pitch black hole." She became thoughtful for a few minutes and then spoke as if she was miles away. "Old clay bricks on the floor and wall, falling apart, almost crumbling when I touched them."

Rico swung her head and glanced at the far away look that Shawn had on her face, looking back to the road, she began to think aloud. "Martinsburg Brick Company, quarry town, abandoned houses…holy shit! Shawn do you remember any structures like out buildings or anything when you were walking?"

Shawn thought for a few moments and then shook her head. "Sorry Rico, the only thing I remember seeing was a pile of old grey lumber. I don't know where it was or anything." She watched as a grin formed on Rico's face.

"That's OK, I'll get a chopper to fly over the area and see if they can spot it. It'll narrow our search area down a bit anyway." She pulled the Blazer in to the parking lot of the FBI building, getting out she walked around to Shawn's side, opened the door for her, and then helped her out. She pointed to a side door and walked towards it with Shawn right on her heels. Shawn looked around nervously, she hadn't been anywhere near people except for Rico's mama, Bobby and Bridget. She stayed in mama's Tracker when they went to the parts store, so this was a little overwhelming for her. She quickly caught up to Rico and took her hand in a tight grip. As they walked down the hall, an atom wouldn't be able to get between their bodies. Shawn wished that she could crawl inside of Rico. Rico felt her discomfort, wrapped an arm around her shoulders, and pulled her close to her side. She didn't even think of how Shawn would take being around so many strange people. She could kick herself for not telling her ahead of time. When they passed people in the hallway, she felt Shawn tremble against her. Dropping her head down near her ear, she whispered comforting words to her, after a few moments she felt her relax a little. Rico stopped outside a solid wooden door with her name on a brass plaque. Using her keys, she opened the door and led Shawn into her office. "Go ahead and make yourself comfortable." She pointed to a soft leather couch and a small refrigerator near the wall. "I don't have any goat's milk." She shuddered at the thought of Shawn drinking the stuff. "But I have other stuff in there, including microwave food."

"Maybe later, I think I'm just going to sit over here and try and find my nerves. I think they freaked and ran off down the hallway   somewhere."

"I'm sorry about not warning you about all the people, I'm so used to being around all the asses that I ignore them." She shrugged her shoulders then went to sit behind her massive oak desk. Turning her PC on, she waited for it to boot up. In those few minutes, she watched Shawn across the room. A warmth grew inside her when she saw her fidget on the couch, she reminded her of a small child that didn't know quite what to do with herself. Opening a desk drawer, she pulled out a mass of chains, bars and other steel objects that were all connected together in a jumbled mess. "Shawn catch." She tossed the mess to her and watched a state of confusion wash over her face.

"What is it?" She held the thing up and turned it in her hands.

"It's a puzzle, you have to get all that untangled and then it'll   come   apart."

66

"And I'll be 200 years old before I figure it out huh?"

"Nah, I did it in twenty minutes." She gave her a crooked grin and winked.

"That's not fair Rico; you just put a time limit on me." She pouted but went ahead and tried to figure out the puzzle. Rico held back the chuckle that wanted to come out at the look on Shawn's face. Looking at the screen of her PC, she typed in her password and grinned when Xena's war cry signaled that her password was accepted. Shyly she looked over the edge of the monitor and saw Shawn with a raised eyebrow looking at her. "Sorry." She ducked her head back down and started typing like a maniac. Minutes later, she was pulling up all the men who were associated with the Nazi's in the surrounding states. Hitting the print button, she heard her printer kick on and start spitting out their files. Upon hearing the rattle of the puzzle, she looked over the monitor and smirked at a frustrated Shawn. It had taken her weeks to figure out the puzzle, she just wanted to have some fun at Shawn's expense. At the heavy pounding on the door, she minimized the screen and yelled for them to enter at their own risk; that got a snort from a grinning Shawn. She had never seen Rico in action so she was in for a big surprise. The door swung open to reveal a platinum blonde in a dark suit that looked like all she had on was the jacket. Without looking anywhere but at Rico, she sauntered across the office and posed seductively on the edge of Rico's desk. With a disgusted look on her face, Rico leaned back in her chair and cast a bored expression on her face. "What do you want Calamari?"

"It's Cassandra, and you know what I want." She ran a finger up Rico's sleeve and laughed when the arm was yanked away.

"Yeah rabies' and tetanus shot."

"How about if you drop your pants and I'll give you a shot of something?" She spread her legs open to show that she wore nothing but a garter beneath her skirt. Her back stiffened when a low snarling noise came from right behind her, slowly, she turned her head and saw furious green eyes and a snarling mouth mere inches from her. "Jesus where the hell did you come from...better yet, what are you?" She said with a haughty air.

"I was just released from Fort Meade women's penitentiary; I haven't had a blonde bimbo in five years!" She crept closer to Cassandra and sniffed at her. "I smell a bitch coming into her period; I love the taste of blood." She licked her lips and smacked them. Whatcha say I chew on ya a little bit?" She flicked her tongue close to the woman's ear and watched her fall off the desk trying to get away from her.

"Rico help me!" She yelled as she crawled away from Shawn. "What is she doing in here?" She asked from where she was now standing on the opposite side of the desk eyeing Shawn. Rico reached out and pulled Shawn onto her lap, placed a soft kiss on her lips, pulled her against her body and raised an eyebrow at Cassandra. "What do you think she's doing here?" She gave her a seductive look and nuzzled Shawn's neck.

"But   she's   so...thin!"

"She got this way from hours of uninterrupted calisthenics with me in my bed." They watched an envious look cross the blonde's   face   then   anger   take   over.

"You're lying Rico; I know you don't date...period! I've tried everything to get you!" She moved a little closer and bent over   showing   her   cleavage.   "Prove   it!"

Rico arched an eyebrow at her. "Sorry, I don't have one of our   VCR   tapes   with   me."

"Then do something easy like...kiss her." A wicked grin covered her face; she knew she had her now, Rico would never show any kind of emotion at the work place. Rico gently turned Shawn so that she was straddling her thighs, lacing a hand behind her neck; she drew her closer to her. Trailing her tongue across Shawn's bottom lip and then between where they had parted a little, she pulled her bottom lip between her teeth and teased it with her tongue. When a low moan came from Shawn, she brought their lips together in a slow exploring kiss. When she felt soft lips part beneath hers, she slowly slipped her tongue into Shawn's mouth and caressed the inside in a way that had both of them moaning. Even after the slam of the office door, they continued to explore each other's mouths until the kiss broke and they clung to each other gasping for air. Shawn leaned her head on Rico's muscular shoulder and tried to catch her breath.

Her voice deep and ragged, Shawn spoke close to Rico's ear.   "My...Gods   Rico   that   was..."

"Yeah it was." Rico replied before she pushed Shawn away from her shoulder and captured her lips once again for a mind-spinning kiss. They both jumped apart when Gabrielle's voice came from the speakers asking them if they wanted a piece of her. Neither one of them could hold back the blush nor the light chuckle at the ideas that were running through their minds. "How about I finish up here and I take you out to eat?"

"I take it that you're not mad at me for scaring squid woman?"

"Nope not at all." She gave her a brilliant smile then one last kiss before she went back to getting the files that she needed.

***

The waiter gave them a funny look when they both sat on the same side of the bench at *TGI Fridays,* Rico gave him a narrowed eyed look and he scampered off with their orders. "How long has squid woman been after you?" Shawn asked as she   popped   a   breaded   mushroom   into   her   mouth.

"Ohh five or six years, she thinks if she gets in my bed, then   she'll   get   promoted."

"How much more asinine can one be, what's wrong with working   for   a   position?"

"It's the work part she doesn't like; she got to where she is by   spreading   her   legs."

"Shows men are pigs." She took a bite out of a potato skin covered in cheddar cheese, bacon bits and sour cream. A deep moan rumbled in her chest and raised Rico's temperature by ten degree's. Rico was struggling to keep from adding her own moan. She had no idea what was happening to her, she, by her rules stayed away from relationships of any kind. With each little moan or groan from Shawn, she felt her rules becoming stupider by the second. She was saved from making an ass of herself in front of the other customers by their waiter bringing the rest of their food. If he hadn't shown up, she knew she would have given Shawn something entirely different to moan about. Rico was leaning back on the bench rubbing her full stomach and was surprised to see Shawn finishing what she had left on her plate.

"Mama's stretched your stomach to the size of a Volkswagen."

"You're lucky; it used to be the size of a semi truck trailer. I was banned from the all you can eat buffet at a restaurant in Dallas." She gave Rico's stomach a rub and grinned when a deep groan came from her tall friend.

"Let's get out of here, you drive and I'll run behind OK?"

***

The weeks went past with Rico leaving a sexually frustrated Shawn at home in the mornings with mama and Jed while she was out in the field trying to find the place where she had been kept for so many months. It was like looking for a needle in a haystack. The grasses and weeds had taken over the fields, obscuring all beneath it. Honeysuckle hung from the trees like vines in the darkest of jungles. They had taken to carrying machetes with them to cut back the overgrowth and to use as protection from the cottonmouth snakes that popped up occasionally. Along with the cuts and scrapes of walking through the untamed vegetation, one agent found not only a rattlesnake but also a beehive on his flight to safety. Medivac chopper flew out him to the nearest hospital for treatment for the countless bee stings. It was beginning to look like they would never find the hidden area and Rico's patience was getting thinner by the day. The time away from searching was spent going over maps, files, old courthouse and land records to find nothing. Shawn and mama were starting to worry about her health, she was thinner and dark circles ringed her blue eyes. She had given Shawn a leather bound journal to write in to help with her memories and nightmares that she had on occasion, but she wouldn't take a day off from the search to take care of her self or let anyone else do it. The straw broke the camels back one morning when Rico was in the kitchen getting up from the table after a hurried cup of coffee. She stood up, took two steps back and hit the floor face first. Adrenaline pumping through her veins, Shawn quickly picked

70

her up and carried her to the couch in the living room leaving a gapping mama to stare after them. With the amount of food and working out in Rico's gym in the basement, she had gone back up to her normal 135 lbs. However, what she had now was solid muscle. The times that Bobby and Bridget came over, she had to beat Bridget off from feeling her biceps and shoulders. Now she was thankful for the strong body, carrying six foot of dead weight was a still a strain on her small compact body. Laying her gently on the couch, she used the bottom of her shirt to wipe the blood pouring from Rico's nose. It didn't look broke but the amount of blood was scary non the less. Shawn stepped back when mama placed an ice bag across the bridge of Rico's nose, after she gave the swelling feature a good crack that had Shawn wincing.

"It was broke wasn't it?" Shawn asked as she wiped more blood from Rico's upper lip.

"Just a little, not the first time I set her nose." Shawn gave her a surprised look, she had studied Rico so intently, that she could recall the smallest detail just by closing her eyes. She couldn't tell that Rico's nose had been broken before. "Get good at settin 'em when ya have five brothers who're all boxers." She adjusted the ice pack and shook her head. "Maybe this will slow her down, if not, I gots lotsa rope in the garage. Use it to if I have ta, stubborn dam lass." She left Shawn to stare at her back as she went into the bathroom and came back with a little brown bottle of mystery. Before opening the lid, she took a deep breath and held it. Waving the bottle under Rico's nose, she jumped back when a large hand swatted at her.

"Mama hates that stuff." She said with a garbled voice. "Nasty smelling shit." She pulled the ice bag from her face and looked around the room. "How did I get here and why do I have ice on my head?" Shawn sat on the edge of the couch and glared at her.

"Because oohh Xena Warrior Princess wannabe, you took a nose dive literally on the kitchen floor. And me being the butch bitch that I am carried your heavy ass in here." She pushed Rico none to gently back onto the couch. "Don't you move or I'll tie you down."

"I don't think you're big enough to stop me wee bit."

Shawn raised an eyebrow at her and snorted. "Right, we'll see about that." She pounced onto Rico's stomach and sat there pretending not to here Rico's struggle for air. "What did you say?" She looked down into a bright red face that was gasping for air and trying to speak. Tilting her head sideways, she cupped her ear with her hand. "Did I hear you say CPR?" Moving so that she stretched out on top of Rico, she put her elbows on her chest, laced her hands together and dropped her chin down on them to stare into watering blue eyes. "Sooo are you gonna stay where you're at or am I..." Was all she was able to say before she was pulled up a tall body to have her lips captured in a kiss that stole the very breath from her lungs. She felt long fingers steal in to her hair, move down across her back, and massage her bunching muscles. A deep moan came from one of them but at the moment neither one of them cared which one. Moving one hand under Rico's back, the other gripped the back of her head and pulled her closer. Sliding a thickly muscled thigh between longer ones, Shawn pushed against Rico's center and felt her hips thrust upward against her. A deep rumbling growl came from Rico right before she flipped them over onto the couch so that Shawn was now   trapped   below   her.

"I see ya not as hurt as I thought." Mama was standing beside the couch with her hands on her hips. "But if ya two keep that up, someone's bound ta gets hurt. Can't even see wee bit under there." She busted out laughing when Rico gave her the "Look". "Don't work on me, Ya got that look from me wee one." She looked closer at her and pointed to her nose. "You're bleedin on   wee   bit."

"Shit!" She rolled off onto the floor and tilted her head back on the couch. She felt Shawn move under her so that her head   was   resting   in   her   lap.

"Here's a towel for the big dummy's nose. Now wee one keeps your head back till it stops." Mama handed Shawn the towel and went back in the kitchen laughing up a storm.

Taking on an Irish accent, Shawn whispered close to Rico's ear. "It's OK wee one; I'll takes care of ya. Can'ts have yas bleedin   ta   death."

"I cans think of other ways of dying." Rico mumbled from

under the towel and ice pressed to her swollen nose. "So ya carried me in here did ya?"

"Uhh huh and I think I strained something afterwards." She leaned down and placed a kiss on Rico's forehead. "Want me to massage it for ya?"

"Hmmm…well, if you massage my strained area, you'll be doing it all night." He voice dropped to a low growl at the end.

"Does your back hurt that bad?" Rico asked then immediately felt stupid when she felt Shawn lift her hips. "Guess that part seems to be a little tender on both of us. Must be contagious."

"But curable." Shawn leaned over and bit the top of Rico's ear, then traced it with her tongue. "Guess I'll go cure this by taking a cold shower." She got up and left a frustrated Rico sitting on the floor.

"Guess I deserve it?" She said to herself, they had only gotten to the stage of a kiss every now and then but the soft caresses that were a constant in their everyday life was enough to ignite a forest fire at this point. Rico was scared to death to do anything about her feelings. Just looking at Shawn had her libido doing a happy dance only to be slapped down by the thought of Shawn one day leaving to go back to her life in Texas. It made her heart grow heavy every time her mom called to talk to her, she never asked what they talked about but the look on Shawn's face when she hung up the phone, was enough to tell her that her mom wanted to know when she was coming back home. She didn't want to mention anything, fearing that if she did, it would bring the day closer. Everyday when she went out into the fields, she wanted to find that hole in the ground and then on the other hand, she didn't. She didn't know what to do, she was damned if she did and damned if she didn't. She looked up when she felt the couch sink next to her head.

"What's wrong wee one?" Mama asked as she brushed her dark bangs back from her bruised forehead.

Tears formed in her eyes. "I'm worried mama."

"About what, Shawn?" She tugged on Rico's hand for her to get off the floor.

"About when this is over…will she leave?" Tears flowed

over her lashes to trail down her cheeks.

"Have ya asked her what she's gonna do?" She snorted when Rico shook her head. "Don't cha think asking would solve that problem? Better yet, tell her what's in your heart."

"What's in my heart won't keep her from going back to her   family."

Mama pulled her into her arms and held her like she did when she was little. "It won't? Then how comes we traveled across the water ta come here ta be with you papa. Do ya think if I didn't love him, we would've stayed in Ireland while he was here?" She placed a kiss on Rico's temple. "I would've gone anywhere's he said ta be by his side. Shawn is a stubborn lass, if ya gives her a reason ta stay, she'll fight the devil himself ta do it. Tell her wee one." She rocked her daughter for a while before telling her to get her ass up and talk with Shawn or she would kick her ass. "Remember, true love is somethin that only comes once   in   a   lifetime."

"How do I know if..."

"Jericho, look in your heart and her eyes and ya'll find your answer. Now get, I didn't raise no coward." Mama left her standing there running her hands through her disheveled hair. She didn't know what to do with her dense child, kicking her in the ass would help with her frustrations of her daughter's foot dragging. But wouldn't do a bit of good for Rico. *"If she don't do somethin, I'll grab Shawn."* She said to herself and then grinned as she closed the kitchen door.

***

Shawn lay on the bed with a towel wrapped around her body, even the cold shower did nothing to douse the flames that danced in her veins. For weeks now, she had been suffering from sensory overload. Just watching as Rico slept had her panting like a bitch in heat, what surprised her was that she didn't develop carpel tunnel Syndrome in her right hand and was glad that the old wives tale about blindness was just a tale or she would be needing a seeing eye dog. After finding out that her mother had kept her checking and savings account active, she had mama take her to Wal-Mart where she bought the best shower massager they had. She gave up on trying to out wit the older woman as to why she wanted one, the minute she mentioned one mama grinned like a lunatic with knowledge. Picturing in her mind, the way Rico looked as she came from the shower with her hair still wet and droplets of water running down across her towel covered body, had her twitching. Running her hand across her breasts, she could feel her nipples grow hard beneath her palm and a light twitch to her center. Pulling the towel apart, she cupped her one breast, ran a thumb across the hardened nipple, and let out a low moan. Her eyes closed as her other hand moved in slow circles across the lower part of her belly, just brushing her damp curls. Bending her knees, she planted her feet on the bed and let her hand explore lower into her wetness. Letting her mind take over, she imagined that it was Rico touching her. She moaned deeper and whispered Rico's name. Rico stopped inside the doorway, frozen in place by what she saw. Her mouth went dry, heart slammed in her chest, wetness pool between her thighs and a whimper escaped from between her lips. From the way Shawn was laying on the bed, she could see her defined stomach muscles ripple when she moved her hips. She was about to turn tail and run to the furthest corner of her property when she heard Shawn speak.

"I need you Rico." Came from between her moist lips, slowly she pulled her t-shirt over her head and dropped it to the floor, unfastening her Levi's she let them puddle around her ankles until she stepped from them and walked on silent feet to the bed. Brushing her fingertips from Shawn's ankles to inner thighs, she leaned forward to place a soft kiss above her soft curls. When she looked up, she connected with dark green eyes surrounded by an embarrassed face. Crawling over Shawn's body, she hovered over her for a few seconds before leaning down to kiss her gently. When she pulled back, she looked deeply into Shawn's eyes and felt her heart skip a beat. "I'm in love with you." She whispered in a deep voice. "From the first moment I looked into your eyes, you had my heart." Rico felt small hands wrap around her neck and pull her down to waiting lips; her breath was stolen the second she felt a warm tongue pass between her lips. The kiss was slow and filled with a passion that Rico had never felt before. When they came apart, she looked into misty green eyes and felt her heart contract. She just knew that she had made a mistake by telling Shawn how she felt.

"You worry too much Rico." Shawn placed soft kisses at the corners of her mouth, keeping within a distance of a shared breath, she whispered to her. "You fill my every waking moment; my dreams at night are of you. I'm in love with you Jericho Chamaune." She pulled Rico down and kissed her until both of them were close to passing out from lack of air. Rico could feel the wetness coating the insides of her thighs and a fullness envelope her nether lips. Laying her body on top of Shawn, she kissed and nipped at the soft skin of Shawn's neck. Feeling the roar of her blood throb against her lips, she licked the pulse point and then nipped and sucked the area until Shawn was whimpering and clutching at her strong shoulders. She left a trail of kisses across her neck and down her chest to stop at the top of her right breast. Placing butterfly kisses around her hardened nipple, she felt her head being pulled down closer to where Shawn wanted her. With the tip of her tongue, she circled her nipple and finally flicked the sensitive end with her tongue. Rolling the other one between thumb and forefinger, she felt strong legs wrap around her hips and a wet center push into her stomach. Gasping at the feel, she pressed her thighs together to try to control her body. Pulling Shawn's nipple between her lips, she sucked and bit hard enough to hear a small gasp from her lover. Moving her lips downward between her breasts, she felt Shawn's legs loosen from around her. Using her fingertips alone, she let them wander across sweat dampened flesh and felt goose bumps rise across Shawn's skin. Sitting up on her calves, she ran her fingertips down from her breasts to her stomach where she trailed them across damp curls. The entire time she held green eyes with her own. Moving backwards down the bed, she lay between muscular thighs, ran her fingers through damp curls, and then down to cover her fingers with her lovers wetness. Bringing her fingers up to her mouth, she reached out with her tongue and took her first taste. A deep moan rumbled from her chest when Shawn opened her legs further and surrendered herself to her.

Keeping eye contact, she ran her tongue across swollen lips slowly. With the flat of her tongue, she teased her lover until she was begging and pushing her head down. Using two fingers, she spread her folds and licked the inside of each nether lip of its juices. Leaving her center for last, she flicked her tongue against it and felt it open beneath her. Placing two fingers right at the edge, she slowly pushed them in to the first knuckle, took the hardened ridge between her lips, and flicked the very tip of it with   her   tongue.

Shawn felt her body quiver from her lover's attentions; no one had ever taken her so slowly towards the top. Her entire body was on fire and in need of release, she could feel her insides tighten around Rico's fingers and then convulse when they were pushed all the way in and wiggled inside of her. She braced her heels into the bed and pushed her center into her lovers face, unintelligible words flowed from her lips as she came closer to the abyss. Rico swirled her tongue around her lover's clit, then sucked hard as she worked her fingers inside of her silken walls. When her fingers were clutched tightly, she tipped them upward, dragged her teeth across her clit, and felt her go over the edge. A loud grunt and then her name came screaming from her lover's lips. Before the pulses stopped, Rico pulled her fingers out, slipped her tongue inside of her, and took her back over the edge. When the tremors stopped, she licked the last of the juices from her and crawled up her body to lay with her head tucked against her sweat soaked neck. Wrapping her arms around her she whispered into her small ear how much she loved her. They lay wrapped in each other's arms for long moments, each trying to catch their breaths and calm trembling bodies. Rico was yet to feel her release; she could feel the fullness between her legs and the slickness of her arousal coating the insides of her thighs. She groaned against her lover's neck when she moved her leg and felt the warmth of her lover's thigh brush her swollen clit. Small hands pushed on her shoulders so that she was lying on her back, Shawn slid her body against hers until she was lying on top of her and looking down into eyes that were almost black in color from arousal. Pressing a kiss to each eyebrow, Shawn moved her way down and across high cheekbones until; she came to slightly bruised lips. Her kiss was slow and seductive, raising both of their temperatures to boiling. After the kiss broke, she nipped and sucked at the moist skin of Rico's neck. Pulling on the softness until a whimpering sound came from Rico's chest.

"You have no idea what you do to me Rico." She straddled Rico's hips and rubbed her wetness against the soaking wet mound. It caused a shuddering to roll through the tall woman's body signaling her climax.

"Ohhh Gods I'm coming!" Rico sobbed as her hips thrust upward to meet Shawn's wetness, her back arched, large hands gripped Shawn's hips and pulled her tighter as her climax over took her in rolling waves. The feel of Rico's hot juices pouring from her contracting center sent Shawn over the edge again. Their combined orgasms were like a volcano erupting, they thrust together melding their centers for mind-blowing shared climaxes. With the last of the tremor's racing through their bodies, Shawn collapsed on top of Rico's sweat covered body. Resting her face on a rapidly rising chest, she hung on for dear life as their bodies once again went into spasms from the press of their thighs against sensitive mounds. All that filled the room were the sounds of heavy breathing. Long minutes later, with the cooling of heated skin, green eyes opened to look upward into the slack face of her lover. Brushing Rico's wet bangs back from her forehead, Shawn noticed that her breathing had returned to its normal rate but was deep as if she were sleeping. Softly kissing the area between her breasts still damp with sweat, she rolled off her to lay by her side. Tracing a dark brow with one finger, she trailed a bead of sweat down her temple and was surprised when Rico didn't move. Lifting one eyelid, she saw nothing but white.

"You passed out on me?" A huge grin broke across her face, and then vanished when she realized that she didn't remember anything but the dancing of brightly colored lights and then calm darkness. "Her features changed to one of shock when she realized that she to had passed out for a time." Gods that has never happened to me before." She rested her head on a strong shoulder and sighed.

"Am I dead?" A deep throaty voice asked close to her, and sent shivers across her skin bring about a tingling in a newly aroused   area.

"Not yet, but if you're feeling anything like I am right now," She pressed her wetness into Rico's hip and moaned. "We will be in a few minutes." Hours passed as they tried to quench their desires, until complete exhaustion and dehydration took their tolls on them and forced them into dead to the world sleep. The next morning, they were roused from oblivion, when the shades were drawn back and the window fan was turned on high. Groggily two sets of eyes traveled to find a smirking mama looking   down   at   their   tangled   bodies.

"OK, ya nymphos' rise and shine. It's ten am and time ta gets in the shower, ya smell like over sexed whore's ya does." With that, she slapped her daughter's bare ass and laughed all the way to the kitchen. Before she stepped through into the room, she yelled back to them. "Hopes ya two got laryngitis after all that screaming this mornin." She had been in the kitchen early that morning and had spilled a fresh cup of coffee on the table when their screams of each other's names scared the hell out of her. She waited an hour before she ventured to their bedroom and was shocked further to see Shawn with her face buried between Rico's thighs. She felt the heat work its way up her face and her heart flutter in her chest enough to feel like a heart attack. She had jumped back from the doorway and taken a nice long walk in the cool morning air. She may be old but she certainly wasn't dead, and that site was enough to remind her. When she heard, the mumbling and then the shower turn on, she grinned. Yelling so that they could here her. "Ya two got fifteen minutes in there then I flush the toilet!" From the first time she met Shawn, she knew that Shawn was going to dominate her stoic daughter in the bedroom. Every time their eyes met, Rico turned to jelly right before her. When they came into the kitchen after their shower with pink faces, she knew it wasn't all from the shower. Rico looked down at her shuffling feet while Shawn gave her a wink and sat down at the table. "Little sore this mornin wee one? After all that I'm surprised either one of a can walk without   being   bow   legged."

Rico dropped her head onto the table and moaned, lacing her hands over the back of her head; she stayed that way until she

79

felt a warm hand run from her knee right up to cup her thumping sex. Reaching under the table, she grabbed the small hand and brought it up to hold it down on the table. "Behave Shawn, I think it's worn out." She looked up at her mama when she busted out   laughing   at   her.

Shawn leaned in close to her ear and purred. "Nah, just broken   in."

***

"You whore, put the rope around you now!" He yelled down into the hole and watched as the woman crawled on her hands and knees towards the rope that was dangling near the ground. She had learned the first time to do as he said, after he came down into the hole and beat her for what seemed hours. Her ribs were broke and breathing was something that she wished she didn't have to do. The pain from a small breath was enough for stars to fill her vision and pull her into the arms of darkness. She knew what he was going to do to her once again, would be the last time for her. "Do I have to come down there again?" He yelled again from above and then waited as she tied the rope around her. "Whores deserve nothing but death! Be gone with the demon spawn of your perversions!" He pulled the rope up, when she was above the hole; he grabbed one arm and dragged her over the edge of the hole. "Your death will count among many and grant me a place in the history of pure race!" He punched and kicked the women until she passed out from the pain, his brutality crest with her blood pouring on the ground. Flipping her onto her back, he raped her savagely until he released with a roar. Rolling her unconscious body back into the hole, he re-covered it, straightened his replica of a Storm Troopers uniform and drove away singing the German national anthem. As the sun moved across the sky, a lone ray glinted off the shiny medal that had fallen from his uniform in his rage.

***

Rico grabbed the phone before the answering machine could pick up, she gasped into the phone breathlessly.

"Chamaune."

"Rico its Stan, we got another one."

"Where?"

"Shepherdstown College, two weeks ago."

"Shit! How come we're just now finding out about it?"

"Because some dumbass in the College office forgot to inform the Sheriffs department."

"Who the hell did they report it to?"

"They have cops there, some are full time rent-a-cop, and other's are off duty cops from the area. One of the guys that's been helping us found the report lying around the office."

"OK, can you send it to me via E-mail so I can have a look at it? Did you guys find anything yesterday?"

"Nope as usual, what happened to you? We waited around and when you didn't show, I sent everyone out in the fields."

"I had a little up close and personal encounter with the kitchen floor, mama wouldn't let me leave the house afterwards." She felt like a two year old when Stan started laughing at her.

"House arrest huh? What did you do that she kept you home?"

"Nosedive literally, I have two black eyes and my nose is a little swollen. It's my own damn fault though, my blood sugar dropped and so did I."

"Why don't you take off for a couple days, we can handle it out here and if we find anything then I'll call you ASAP."

"Excuse me but who's the boss here?"

"Right now I am Rico; don't make me call your mama." He threatened and chuckled when Rico mumbled a couple of curses and then agreed after he heard a loud yelp coming from her. *"I guess you're not the boss there either?"*

"Fuck you Stan; I'll see you in a couple of days." She hung up the phone, gave Shawn her most dangerous look for the slap on the ass she had gotten and failed to get even a flinch out of her. "Must be losing my touch, I'll have to practice on Jed or something." She mumbled and then dropped onto the couch and pouted for all she was worth.

Shawn dropped down onto her lap and wrapped her arms around her neck. "I wouldn't say that." She ran a finger across the jutting bottom lip and then nipped it with her teeth. "I happen to love the way you touch." Teasing Rico's lips with her tongue, she waited to gain entrance. When a deep moan came from Rico's parted lips, Shawn thrust with her tongue and dueled with her lover's until she was able to win the fight and push Rico so that she was lying on the couch with Shawn straddling her hips. Hands roamed until bare skin was found beneath clothing, soft moans and groans passed between them. Clothes quickly hit the floor in a pile, overheated bodies moved against each other until the roof was in danger of loosing shingles. They never heard the pitter-patter of little hooves come towards them and then disappear.

***

Mama looked up when Jed ran passed her as she was weeding the garden. Getting up, she followed her goat until she was able to see what she was playing with. Shaking her head, she took the article of clothing from Jed and held it up with both hands to see that they were Rico's *Spiderman* boxers. She knew that not a half hour ago she had been wearing them. "What are you two up to now?" She wondered as she headed towards her daughters house. Sneaking through the house, she stopped in the living room, looked over the back of the couch and saw two naked bodies wrapped around each other in sleep. "Should have known." She dropped the boxers on the pile of clothes and covered them with a thin blanket. "Sex fiends ya are." Her face broke out into a huge smile when she thought about the two women. "Bout damn time someone claimed her." She went back out to her garden to finish weeding before she would make supper for them.

***

Rico was bouncing off the walls, she wasn't allowed in her office to work, all her files had been hidden by mama and Shawn and now she sat on the back deck staring off into the

82

distance wondering if she snuck away if they would notice. She was about to get up out of her chair when she felt two arms wrap around her from behind. "Would you take me somewhere?" Shawn asked in a deep purring voice that had Rico thinking the bedroom. Being a smartass, she asked Shawn. "What's wrong with right here?" She slapped her thighs and thrust her hips upward.

"We'll have plenty of time for that later." She dropped a newspaper into her lap and pointed to the highlighted ad. "Will you take me to see that?"

Rico read the ad and then looked over her shoulder into pleading green eyes. "You want a dirt bike?"

"Uhh huh, and that ones only $500.00 because it needs some engine work. Will you take me…please?" She gave a puppy dog look and watched as Rico sighed and gave in.

"I have something better for you to do than play with that." Blue eyes twinkled down at her. "Come with me wee bit." She took her smaller hand and led her to a shed out behind her mama's house. Swinging the door open, she pulled a tarp off an old motor cycle and watched, as Shawn's eyes grew wide with disbelief. "Will that do?" Shawn ran a hand over the leather seat of the 1971 CB 360 Honda. "Everything is original; I have spare parts for it in that wooden trunk against the wall.

Shawn looked at her and her face broke into a huge grin. "Rico, that's the first over the head cam Honda ever made, are you sure?"

"It's yours if you want it." Her answer came as a small body launching into her and a breath-stealing kiss.

"Thank you, no ones ever given me anything like this before." She gave her one last kiss before beginning her inspection of her new toy. Three days later, after she had pulled the Honda apart, cleaned the pistons, re-set the valves and gapped them and put everything back together. She dropped a new battery into it, turned the key and kicked the engine over. A huge grin covered her face when the engine purred like it did years ago. Kicking it into first gear, she headed out into the open field behind mama's house. Rico came running out of the garage and stood in awe of her lover. A cloud of dust followed behind her as she pulled a wheelie and tore across the field.

"Ya gots your hands full with wee bit." Mama said from beside here.

"Sure do and that's just how I like it."

"Have ya asked her about the future yet?"

Rico's shoulders slumped, shaking her head in the negative; she turned troubled blue eyes to her mama. "Not yet."

"Well wee one, ya better hurry 'cuz her mom called and from the sound of her voice, some things wrong in Texas."

Rico's eyes misted over, shaking her head, she wandered back into the garage to hide her pain from her mama. She sat on her workbench and cried for the unknown and her own cowardice to face it. All she had to do was ask Shawn but she didn't have the courage to do it and know she was suffering deeply. She lost track of time sitting there alone in her pain, it wasn't until Shawn came looking for her that she noticed that it had gotten dark outside. She covered her eyes when the overhead lights came on. "Sorry Rico, I didn't know that you were sitting in here." She walked up and pulled the hands down from Rico's face and saw that her eyes were swollen and red and her face was tear stained. "What's wrong?" She asked, holding larger hands in hers, she placed a kiss on Rico's knuckles.

"Nothing."

"Rico you've been crying, so don't tell me nothings wrong."

Rico's eyes filled with tears and overflowed to run down her cheeks and drip off her chin. "You're leaving aren't you?"

Green eyes grew large; Shawn's mouth worked a few times then closed. She looked down at their joined hands and nodded her head. "I have no choice…" She didn't get to finish her sentence because Rico jumped down from the bench and stormed out of the garage. Shawn threw her hands in the air and bellowed Rico's name.

"God damn it!" She ran after her and caught a hold of her upper arm only to be shrugged off. "You stubbornGoddamnthickheaded DIP SHIT!" Grabbing Rico's hand, she spun her around to face her. "Will you at least let me finish before you run off and act like a two year-old?"

"Why bother, you're leaving and that's the end of it." She tried to walk away again but found a small body throwing her to the ground and holding her there.

"If you would let me finish," She glared down into misty eyes. "I have to go back to sign some papers, collect my transcripts, personal items and then I'm coming back. That is if you want me?" She looked deeply into Rico's eyes for her answer. Rico pulled her down against her chest and sobbed with relief.

***

Days later, they stood in Dulles International Airport waiting for the last call for passengers for Flight 1519 to Denver. Shawn would have to take the connecting trip to Dallas where her mom would pick her up and take her home. They stood so close to each other that a piece of paper couldn't be forced between them. Shawn had tears running down her face while Rico held back her emotions behind her stoic FBI mask. They turned their heads when the last call went over the PA system announcing the final boarding for her flight. She started to walk away when she felt a hand take hers and spin her around to be engulfed in strong arms and pulled up against Rico's body. Her sobs broke loose and she cried into Rico's chest. Giving up on the fight, Rico let the tears flow from her eyes. Leaning back, she lifted her lover's chin and kissed her with all the passion and love she felt in her entire body. When they came apart, Shawn looked into her misty eyes and grinned. "You realize were in public?"

"I don't give a shit, I love you and if they can't handle that then I'll take their names and report them to the IRS."

"I love you Rico." She kissed her one last time before walking towards the customer service agent. She turned when she heard Rico call out her name.

"I'll be here to pick you up on Friday. I love you Shawn."

Shawn blew her a kiss. "I love you to Rico." Rico watched the plane back off the gate and taxi away, her heart felt heavy and darkness invaded her soul as her light took off into the sky. "Be careful wee bit."

After spending hours talking about how she had been kidnapped, held in a pitch black pit and her escape Shawn sat at the kitchen table while her mom fixed supper for them, it had been years since she had been home. The feeling was of being misplaced. Her room was still the same as it had been before she left for college years before, but she didn't think of this as home anymore. Her home was with Rico and nothing could change that. She had been sitting there trying to find a way to tell her mom that she was not staying in Texas, that she was going back to Virginia to make a life with Rico. As of yet, she had no idea of how to tell her without hurting her. "Shawna tell me about these women that you were staying with."

"Well, mama...I mean Marie is a riot, she has this little goat named Jed that thinks it's a dog. She goes every where with her and comes into the house and steals Rico's clothes."

"Rico, who is this Rico?"

She rolled her eyes at her and groaned. "Mom, her name is Jericho but we call her Rico. She's the FBI Director for the Tyson's Corner Branch and my best friend." Her mother had turned to look at her and saw the look in her daughter's eyes when she mentioned Rico. She knew that look and it worried her. "Your best friend or something more Shawna?"

Shawn ran her hands over her face and sighed. "More mom much more," She looked up into her mom's hazel eyes. "She's my lover."

"I want to meet this woman."

Shawn's eyes grew wide and her chin dropped to the table.   "Mom?"

"You heard me Shawna; I want to meet the woman who's captured my daughter."

Mama was ready to call Bobby and have her bring over a sedative to knock her daughters ass out for the next week. She paced back and forth in whatever room she just happened to be in. She didn't sleep and only ate when she was forced to. "If ya don't sit yar ass down I'll knock ya down!" Mama threatened with a finger on Rico's nose. "Ya pacin ain't gonna bring her home no sooner so SIT!"

"Mamaaa." Rico whined before she dropped into the kitchen chair.

"Don't whine, drives me nuts like yar pacin. Dontcha have some work ta do?"

"I can't concentrate, all I can think of is what will I do if she changes her mind."

"Ohh ye of little faith, knock it off. She's comin back." Rico leapt out of her chair when the phone rang, grabbing it up she said.

"Wee bit?"

"Nope, but that's what my wife calls it."

"I bet she does Stan."

"Smartass, anyway I have some news for you. We saw a truck leaving the field about a half hour ago."

"I'm on my way, stay where you are and I'll find you." She grabbed her truck keys and took off out of the house without a word to mama.

***

She tore down the river road and came to a place where she could see the weeds pushed down in the opposite direction than she was sitting. Shifting her Blazer into first gear, she took off down the path and followed it for almost four miles before it came to a fork in the field. Turning to the left, she opened her cell phone and called Stan to tell him what she was doing and for him to look for where the truck he had seen had come from. Continuing on her way, she came to an area that the weeds were all knocked down and only one small path was going off towards the North. Pulling her clip on holster from under her seat, she clipped it to the back of her belt and got out of her Blazer. Stashing her keys up under the running board, she then followed the small path for another half mile before she came to a brush pile. Kicking the debris with a booted foot, she found a concrete slab beneath it. Her heart rate picked up when she realized that she had found the place where Shawn had been kept for over seven months. Pulling her cell phone from her pocket, she was about to call Stan when she was tackled from behind and a rag was forced over her mouth. She fought against the heavy weight on her back until the darkness invaded her mind and she fell unconscious to the ground.

"Got myself a real fighter this time." The uniformed man said as he pulled Rico's pistol from her holster and stuffed it into his belt. Searching her body all he found was a few dollars in her pocket and some loose change. "What are you doing with a gun? Whore's are not to posses anything!" He hauled back his fist and punched her in the face. "You are not to have anything but death!" He continued to punch and kick her until he was gasping for air. Leaving Rico to lay on the ground with her blood flowing from numerous cuts and gashes, he went off into the field, came back with a tow truck chain, and hooked it to the steel ring at the edge of the concrete slab. Going back the way he came, he started up the small electric wench he had attached to a thick tree and pulled the slab from over the pit. Once it was moved enough, he went back to Rico, pushed her through the small opening, and listened for the splash of her hitting the bottom.

***

Shawn and her mom were in the living room watching some stupid program on the TV. She got off the couch and was half way across the room when a sharp pain pierced her chest; she dropped to her knees, clutched her chest and gasped for air. Her mom jumped up from the couch and came to kneel by her side. Pulling her into her arms, she ran her hand across her sweating forehead. Her voice cracking with emotion. "Shawna what's wrong?" Laying her daughter on the floor, she crawled across the floor and grabbed the phone. "I'm call 911." She was about to dial when Shawn pulled on the phone.

"It's...Rico! I have...to call...mama...some things wrong." She gasped out as the pain wracked her body.

"Shawn you need to go to the hospital!" Her mom cried

out as Shawn gasped for air and clutched her chest. "No! Call mama NOW!"

Giving into her daughter's request, she hit the speed dial and waited for it to be picked up on the other end. As soon as she heard Marie, she asked for Rico.

"She's not here, can I take a message?"

"Uhhmm wait a minute Shawna wants to talk to you."

Her voice strained from her chest pains, she forced her voice to sound normal. "Mama where's Rico?"

"Wee bit what's wrong?"

"It's Rico; some things happened to her…I can feel it."

"She went out into the field, Stan called…"

"Mama please."

"Shawn I'll call you back, let me get a hold of Stan and see if she's with him."

"Mama I'm flying back on the next plane." She hung up and crawled to her feet. "Mom I have to go back, Rico's in trouble." She stumbled to her bedroom and threw some clothes into a backpack. She turned when she heard her mother's rapid footfalls head to her own room. A few minutes later, she stepped into her daughter's bedroom holding a small over night bag and her car keys. "Come on Shawna, maybe we can catch the next flight to Dulles."

Green eyes took in the whole picture, she didn't understand. "Mom?"

"Come on lets go, I'm not letting you get in trouble alone."

***

Rico moaned and tried to roll over only to be held in place by a pair of thin arms. She tried to focus her eyes but everything was totally black where she was. Her voice was thick and partially slurred, her jaw hurt so much that when she tried to move it, she saw starbursts in front of her.

"Please don't move, you're all busted up." A soft voice came from the person holding her.

Rico spoke from between her teeth. "Ow ong een ere?"

"It's hard to say, but I'm guessing maybe a day or so." She held Rico tighter against her thin body when she felt her trying to sit up. "It's OK, just stay still, my names Cindy by the way."

"Ave to et out."

"It's impossible, I've tried. We're in some kind of old cistern or something and I think there's concrete above us."

Rico searched her pockets, pulled her cell phone out, and handed it to Cindy. "Ry it." Cindy flipped it open, the small phone lit up but she couldn't get a signal.

"It's no use; I can't get a signal down here. Does anyone know where you are?"

"FBI, lose by."

"The FBI? Why are they, oh my Gods you're an agent." She felt Rico nod her head, a soft sobbing came from Cindy as hope returned to her. "Please God let them find us."

***

Stan was ready to tear the entire State of West Virginia apart since he had received the call from her frantic mama; they had searched the entire area for Rico or her Blazer and couldn't find anything. He himself had driven up and down river road where she had said she was. The only thing he saw were freshly cut fields of hay. He had a chopper fly over the area and they were unable to spot anything from the air. It was coming up on fifteen hours since she had come up missing and time was running out for them to find clues of any kind. He knew that if he didn't find his boss, not only was his career over but his life when mama and Shawn got a hold of him.

***

Shawn was going crazy; they had to take four planes to get to Dulles because of the damn weather in Dallas. She sat and clenched her fists in her lap and watched as they flew over Sterling Virginia towards the landing strip. She had called mama from the air and told her what time they would be landing; mama assured her that she would be right out front of the terminal

90

waiting for them. No sooner had the wheels touched down, that she was pulling her backpack out from under the seat in front of her. Three minutes later when the seat belt light went off, she was out of her seat and charging towards the door that was being opened with her mom hot on her heels. When she came out of the jet way a man in a dark suit grabbed her arm, showed her his FBI badge and escorted her and her mom down the jet way stairs and to a dark sedan that was parked in the envelope.

"Where's Marie?" She asked as they ran towards the car.

"I'm right here Shawn!" She yelled from the open window and pushed open the back door for them. With in seconds they were being escorted by an airport authority's vehicle with lights flashing and sirens howling towards the gate four parking lots. Once they were up onto Rt. 28, three State Highway Police cruisers took off in front of them and escorted them all the way to Rico's front door. The entire ride was in total nervous silence, the three women were lost in their own thoughts as to where Rico was being held. Shawn had been thinking long and hard ever since she had collapsed from the severe chest pains. She knew at that moment that she and Rico had some kind of connection that was unexplainable. She hoped that she could use this bond to find her lover. Before the sedan had come to a complete halt, Shawn was out the door and running for the cabin. Hitting the alarm off, she tore through the door and went to Rico's office. Pulling open the closet door, she grabbed Rico's double shoulder harness, spare ammunition and her badge that hung from a thick chain that was looped over a hook on the door. Pulling it over her head, she put the harness on, stuffed the ammunition clips in her back pockets and then pulled Rico's FBI windbreaker on. Running from the office, she ran past her mom and mama and out to the garage. Before they could catch up to her, she took off down the driveway on her motorcycle.

"Where's she going?" Mrs. MacDonaill asked.

Mama looked at the worried woman, took her by her arm and led her back into the cabin. "To find Rico, that's where wee bits headed. I have ta call Stan and lets him know that the tiny terror is on her way."

"Tiny terror?"

"That's what he's been a callin her since he found out she was comin back. The poor mans scared ta death as it is." They walked into the kitchen; mama pointed to the coffee maker and asked her if she would make a fresh pot while they waited.

"Sure, by the way, my names Rita. Who are we waiting for if you don't mind me asking?"

"Bobby and Bridget, they're friends of Shawn and Rico. They treated Shawn when she was found and we'll need them here for when Shawn finds Rico."

"How can you be sure that she'll find her?"

"I just have this feelin and I'm never wrong when it comes ta me gut."

***

"She's WHAT!" Stan yelled over his cell phone. "Just what I need a crazed lover out here driving me nuts!"

"Now Stan ya knows we can't handle either one of them, so ya just gots ta deal with it."

"Ohh for Christ sakes! I swear when I find your daughter I'm going to plant my foot up her ass!"

"Get in line Stan, Shawn's first."

***

Rico was able to sit up and lean against the wall of their prison, her face hurt so bad that she was sick to her stomach; her ribs ached making her believe that some of them were cracked if not broken and her one arm was broken for sure. Even in her condition, she knew that she would kill the son of a bitch when he showed up. She knew that he would, from what Cindy had told her, he was coming out everyday to beat and rape her. All they could do now was wait for him to show, with the two of them, they would have a better chance of at least one of them getting free. For a few seconds her heart rate sped up and made her think that she may be having a heart attack. She grabbed her chest and waited for the pains to pass only to have a feeling of something akin to nervousness. "Shawn." She whispered to herself. *I'm so sorry Shawn, I love you wee bit.* She said to herself as silent tears flowed down her face to soak her damp shirt. Deep down inside, she knew that her lover was coming for her, she hoped that it wasn't to late when she did.

***

Shawn flew down Rt. 9 like a bat out of Hell, her eyes watering from the sharp wind cutting in behind her sunglasses. She heard a siren behind her and knew that a cop was after her for numerous traffic violations, one of them being that she was doing over 90mph in a 55 zone. She hoped that he could keep up with her because she had a feeling that she would need his help before long. Down shifting so fast that she was thrown towards the handlebars, she made the turn onto river road so sharp that she dragged the foot pegs across the asphalt and shot sparks from them. Shifting up into fifth gear, she was back up to almost 65mph when she took the next curve so sharp that a drag racer would be envious. Her heart skipped a beat as she came near a small grove of trees by the railroad tracks ahead of her. Slowing down, she went over the tracks and disappeared into the trees.

***

The large truck bounced along the edge of the railroad tracks, the driver had to go a different way so that the men out in the fields searching didn't see him. He had picked a spot so covered that they couldn't see it from the air and after he had cut the hay fields, they couldn't see his path unless they were on their knees. This would be the last time he came out here, after this, he would move on to other killing fields in other states. It was too risky here for his mission and he couldn't stop until he was through vanquishing the world of the sexual perversions. He looked down at his dashboard clock and saw that he had maybe three hours before dark. It wouldn't take him that long to kill the women, but he wanted to take his time with the tall dark one. From the way she was built, he knew that she was a chosen one and would need special attention. Coming up on a risky hill, he slowed his huge truck down to a crawl and eased it over the hill at an angle. Once it was safe to park it with out fearing that it would roll over onto its side, he got out and started walking.

***

"OK mama what's the emergency about this time?" Bridget asked as she walked into the living room with Bobby behind her.

"Rico's missing; we think that maniac that had Shawn has her now."
Both women's faces went pale; Bobby slumped against her wife and would have fallen if not for a strong arm going around her waist.

"How? I mean where was she?" Bobby asked.

"She was out in the fields searchin and never come home or called Stan or me." Looking to Rita, she introduced the two women and noticed the shocked look on her face when she said the word wife when introducing Bobby.

"I guess I need to get used to this. It's just that where we're from it's not seen."

"We understand Mrs. MacDonaill; I hope we aren't making you uncomfortable." Bobby said as she took a seat on the couch next to mama. "It took our parents a while to get used to it."

"I'm fine don't worry about it. You treated Shawn after she was found I've been told. How bad was she?"

"Where is she anyway?" Bridget asked mama.
"Guess?"

"Ohh shit! She's out there looking for Rico." She dropped her head into her hands and sighed deep in her chest. "I feel sorry for who ever comes in contact with her."

"Why's that?" Rita asked and was told about how she had terrorized all of the hospital personnel and the rest of the story about her short stay at the hospital. Rita sat there with her mouth hanging open, the young women they were describing was not the daughter she had raised. She had no idea that Shawna could be so vicious. Know she had an idea of why the FBI assistant director called her the tiny terror. The women sat in the living

94

room waiting for some word from any one; they were all worried sick and just wanted one small bit of information to go on.

***

Shawn took off across a field once she was out of the small grove of trees, she had started in one direction at first but it didn't feel right to her. Turning around, she went in the opposite direction and felt a tingling in the pit of her stomach. Slowing down, she kept her eyes on the ground looking for a sign. It came to her on the air, a load rumbling noise that sparked a memory. Gunning the throttle, she popped up over a small hill and saw the truck ahead and then the man dressed in a black uniform jacket, she couldn't see the rest of him because he was walking down an incline. It didn't matter, she knew who he was by the sick feeling in her stomach. Tearing across the field, she flew up over the hill he had disappeared from and saw him no more than ten feet in front of her. When he turned, she headed right for him. Down shifting into fourth gear, she popped the clutch and gunned the throttle until the front end came up off the ground. She felt the impact and was thrown from the Honda when it hit him square in the chest. Lying on the ground, she tried to catch the breath that had been forced from her lungs. With each small breath, she felt a sharp pain but forced it down as she rolled over from her back and got to her knees. Looking to where her Honda was lying on its side with the engine still running, she saw his black goose boots sticking out from underneath it.

"Mother fucker!" She grumbled as she made it to her unsteady legs and tried to walk over to him. "I'm going to kill you for what you did to me and Rico." When she made it over to him, she saw that he was unconscious and not going anywhere soon. Stumbling in the direction that he was headed, she scanned the area ahead looking for the trap door she knew had to be there somewhere. She came to a small copse of trees, closing her eyes; she leaned against one to catch her breath. Her pulse picked up and raced through her body, stepping around the tree, she tripped over the base and found the chain lying in a heap by her feet. Looking around her, she saw the brush pile. Picking up the end of the chain, she saw that it had a huge hook on the end. Dragging it towards the brush, she kicked at the edge and found the steel ring. Attaching the hook, she ran back to the tree and found the electric winch. Flipping it on, she heard the loud scrape as it pulled the concrete slab back from the pit. When it was all the way clear, she turned it off and ran over to peer down into the darkness. "RICO!" She yelled and heard a soft voice from below.

"Help us please!" Cindy cried softly.

"Let me find a rope and I'll throw it down to you!" She went to the slab and started moving the brush aside looking for rope or something to throw down to the woman. She knew that he would keep something close to the area; she just had to find it. Coming up empty, she went back to the tree where the winch was, searched the base, and found the rope hanging from a low branch. Low for Rico, a mile high for her. She jumped and still couldn't reach it, finding a stick she tried to get a hold of it but was still to short. Her temper flared, she threw the stick with all her strength and watched as it bounced off the tree and hit the rope knocking just enough down that she was able to jump up and grab it. Running back to the pit, she lowered the rope down and yelled to the woman.

"Are you the only one down there?" Her heart skipped when she heard a deep grunt and then a moan. "Rico? Gods I found you." Tears started flowing from her eyes and blurring her vision. "Wrap the rope around you and I'll help you up."

"She's hurt real bad! I don't think she'll be able to help you!" Cindy yelled up to her. "Please hurry he might show up!"

"Don't worry about him; just get the rope around Rico!" Rico could barely stand the pain that shot through her body made her head spin and whistles go off in her head. She felt the rope being tied around her chest and flinched when it was drawn taught.

"Please be careful with her, she has broken ribs!" Cindy yelled up to Shawn.

"I'll kill him if he isn't all ready dead!" She mumbled to herself as she planted her feet and started to pull the rope hand over hand. With her entire body straining, hands burning from the coarse rope, she ignored the pain and kept pulling until she saw

96

the top of her lover's dark head come up over the edge. Her body numb, she pulled with all her strength until she had half of Rico's body out off the pit. Crawling over to her, she pulled her the rest of the way out and moved her as gently as she could away from the pit. Tears flowed down her face to mix with sweat and dirt. She couldn't help but sob at the condition of her lover. She was so badly beaten and bloody that she didn't know how she survived as long as she had. She looked up when she heard the voice from her   nightmares.

"You're dead! You died months ago!" The crazed man said from where he stood next to the cement slab. He bent down, grabbed a thick log in his hand, and came towards her. "I'll just have   to   kill   you   again!" A darkness over came her from deep in her soul, dimming out the light that burned there. "MOTHER FUCKER!" Shawn screamed as she ran towards him and tackled him to the ground. Knocking the log from his hand, she punched him in the face and heard the crack of bones beneath her fists, she pummeled him until she was gasping for air and he lay there with blood pouring from his nose and mouth. A deep groan came from his split lips as she pushed off his chest and stood on trembling legs. Moving back towards Rico, she didn't hear him get to his knees or the click of the hammer being pulled back on the ancient German pistol he had in his hand. She saw pale blue eyes widen and a limp hand motion behind her. As she spun, she pulled Rico's Glocks from the holsters and opened fire on him as his first shot went off. She didn't stop firing until all she heard was the clicking noises on empty chambers. Falling to her knees, she pressed a hand to her shoulder   and   pulled   away   a   blood-covered   hand. "Son of a bitch!" She mumbled before she crawled on hands and knees to Rico. Leaning over her, she placed a soft kiss to her split, cracked lips and then whispered in her ear. "I love you wee one. Just hold on for me." She untied the rope and dropped it back down into the pit for the other women.

***

Stan called a halt when he heard all the gunshots off in the distance. Yelling for one of the sheriffs that had a quad runner, he jumped on the back and pointed in the direction that the shots had come from. He just hoped that the shots didn't mean that his boss was dead or Shawn. They bounced across the field in the dimming light, the bright headlight skimming the ground before them. The sheriff was about to stop when his headlight caught movement off to the side. Stan gripped his shoulder and pointed to where he saw a small form stumbling away from them. He jumped from the back of the quad and ran towards the person who had just turned around and raised two pistols and pointed them at him. He stopped and raised his hands over his head. "Shawna! It's Stan!"

"Ohh Gods! I need help Rico's hurt bad!" She yelled and dropped to her knees in exhaustion and relief. She was on her way to get the huge truck and try to get them to the hospital. With Stan there, she crawled back to her lover and collapsed to the ground at her side. She pulled Rico's head onto her shoulder and let her tears run down her cheeks and into dark hair. Cindy was sitting next to them with her knees under her chin and her arms wrapped around her knees. Tears ran down her face from the sheer joy of being alive, she knew that she would never be the same after what had happened to her but knew that she would always owe her life to both women. If Rico had not been thrown into the hole with her, she knew that Shawn would never have come searching and found them both. She now knew the feeling of undying love and the connection that could be present between two people. One day she hoped to find someone who could connect so deeply with her the way Rico and Shawn had. Stan dropped to his knees beside the women, pulling a flashlight from his pocket; he placed a piece of cloth over the lens so that the bright light wouldn't blind them. He gasped when he saw his bosses face.

"Rico you are one hell of a mess." He whispered to himself and jumped when his shirt was grabbed and he was forced down close to her face.

"ou ain't o etty ourelf!"

Stan looked to Shawn with puzzlement showing in his eyes. "Did she just insult me?"

"I'd say so." She chuckled at his gapping expression.

"Just for that, I'm calling your mama." He stuck his tongue out at her and pulled his cell phone out. After a short conversation, he called the sheriff over and sent him for the truck that Shawn had told him was parked a short distance away. "I heard gunshots, was that you?" He looked to Rico and then to Shawn when she grabbed his sleeve and pointed to where the Nazi's body lay crumpled on the ground. "I shot him."

A few hundred times." Cindy said as she pulled Rico's windbreaker tighter around her thin body and then started laughing. "Pissed me off when I found out she didn't save me one so I could shot the son of a bitch." They heard the sound of ambulances off in the distance and then the rumble of the truck as the sheriff drew as close as he could to where they were. Stan scooped a moaning Rico up into his arms and carried her towards the truck. Shawn waited until he had her lover inside before she crawled in after her and pulled her into her arms. Stan went back, helped Cindy to the quad, placed her in front of him, and followed behind the others as they made their way towards the road where the ambulances would be waiting. Stan knew that Rico would be pissed when she found out that she was going to the hospital, but with all the damage done to her and the time spent in the pit, he would fight her tooth and nail if he had to. He hoped that having Bobby, Bridget, mama and most importantly Shawn there would calm her down so that she could be treated.

***

Rico tried to fight the paramedics all the way to the hospital; she ended up being tied down with Shawn whispering in her ear threatening to tell mama how kinky, she was and what they had done on the kitchen table. That calmed her quickly; she didn't want her mama having any more ammunition to hang over her head when she wanted her to do something she detested. When she was wheeled through the ER doors, she couldn't see out of her swollen eyes but she could hear her mama and Bobby talking in one of the treatment rooms. The minute she was pushed in to the room, she heard her mama gasp and felt her hand being taken in her mama's.

"Wee one, what did he do to ya?" She bent forward and placed a kiss on her daughter's forehead. Brushing her blood stiffened bangs back; she caressed her face and whispered close to her ear. "I love you wee one, now you lets Bridget takes care of ya." With tears in her eyes, she kissed her forehead one last time before she left the treatment room and let Bridget do her job. She found Shawn being dragged away from the room by Bobby and Rita pointing a finger at her. She couldn't help but grin when Shawn snarled and snapped at Bobby's hand. "Wee bit behaves and lets her take a look at ya."

"Mama I need to go to Rico!" She yelled as she struggled against Bobby. "I'm not hurt I don't need help!" She tried to push Bobby but found her feet sliding backwards on the tiled floor. "Mama help me!" She pinned her mom with flashing green eyes. "Mom help me!" Rita stopped in the hallway; she raised her chin in the air and tossed her shoulder length blonde hair back. Her one hand planted on her hip, she pointed a finger at her daughter.

"Gets yar ass in there and lets her fix yar shoulder!"

Mama busted out laughing, it was the first time that she heard Rita speak with any kind of accent except a slight Texas drawl. It reminded her of when Rico got frustrated and her true accent came bubbling out.

"Damn it Shawn, I'm about ready to knock your simple ass out!" Bobby said between gritted teeth. "When I'm done with you, then you can see Rico and not until then. Now move your ass!"

***

Rico had been moved to a private room with the exception of all the people filling it. She was covered in numerous bandages over her upper torso and face. Bridget had ended up taking her into the OR to wire her ribs and re-inflate her left lung and then had a plastic surgeon come into suture the numerous cuts and gashes on her face along with resetting her dislocated jaw, re-break and set her nose. She didn't know how she had survived with all of her injuries, she did know that if it had been her down in that pit, she would have died. She also checked on Cindy when they brought her in, she was in bad shape but nothing compared to Shawn when she had been found. She was put in a room down the hall and being just as stubborn as the others are; she had escaped and was now in the room with the Shawn fan club. "OK people, visiting hours are over." She said from the doorway. "You'll can come back in the morning; sleeping beauty there needs her rest." She flinched when ice blue eyes opened to a slit to stare at her. "You're supposed to be asleep."

"Ohh she is." Shawn said as she yawned and her jaws cracked. "She sleeps with her eyes open, scares the shit out of me."

Bridget shivered and rubbed her arms. "She's freaky."

"But she's all mine, freaky sleeping habits and all." Shawn said as she clasped the larger hand in hers and laid her head on the edge of the mattress. With in seconds, her body gave up the battle and her eyes dropped closed.

***

Bridget walked into Rico's room and snorted at the position Shawn was sleeping in. Her head rested back against the bed at a strange angle, legs over the arm of the chair and her right arm stretched across her chest to grip a larger hand in her gauze covered one. She had fought Bobby the entire time when she was trying to scrub the debris and pieces of rope fiber from her torn palms. Now Bridget could see where blood had seeped through the gauze and the swollen fingers gripping Rico's. Slowly walking up to her, she pushed her bangs back from where they covered   her   eyes.

"Shawn, time to wake up." She ran her knuckles across Shawn's cheek and watched her eyes fight to open, a low moan vibrated from her chest and one had grabbed her neck.

"My head's falling off." She whined and tried to rub the

kink out of her neck and shoulders.

"If it does I have a roll of duct tape at the nurse's desk. Come on I have to check on tall dark and bruised. Go get some coffee and something to eat, you look like shit." Her caramel colored eyes twinkled when Shawn growled at her. "Little bull terrier." She grumbled under her breath when Shawn made it to her feet and moved towards the foot of the bed.

A slight accent leaked out as she stood with her arms crossed over her chest. "I ain't leavin, I'm stayin right here."

Casting a look over her shoulder. "Damn leprechauns, suit yourself but I'm warning you it's not nice." Bridget pulled the sheet down from Rico's body, pushed her hospital gown and checked the incision she had made along her ribcage. She looked at Rico's face and saw her eyes opened to a slit but she ignored them. "Damn she heals fast." She ran her fingers across her ribs and jumped when a deep rough voice grunted at her.

"Copping a free feel Bridge?"

"I thought you were asleep, freaky ass bitch." She pulled the gown down and continued to check her other wounds. "How do you feel? I know it's a stupid question but."

Rico raised her cast-covered arm and waved it a bit. "Like shit. Where's wee bit?"

"I'm here, have to make sure doc there doesn't get to friendly with you." She went back over to Rico's side and took her hand in hers.

Rico licked her dry lips and turned her head a little to be able to see her lover; her eyes still swollen but not as much since her nose had been set. She couldn't believe that in less than a couple of months she had her face rearranged twice. She flexed her jaw a few times and only felt a little discomfort. "Pretty ugly huh?"

Tears filled Shawn's eyes when she looked into pale blue.

"Never." Bending over she placed a soft kiss on her dry lips and buried her face against a warm neck.

Bridget rolled her eyes. "Geez wee bit, why don't you just crawl in bed with her." She moved around the other side of the bed and with one arm flipped Shawn up into the bed to lie beside her lover. "No funny stuff you two, you both need sleep and Rico Savvy needs to heal before you can act like rabid weasels."

***

Stan had found a receipt in the Nazi's truck for the Leaning Tree hotel. He along with the sheriffs department headed over there as soon as the body was collected and taken to the morgue. Opening the door, he let out a low whistle as he looked around the small two rooms. On every inch of wall space and around the windows and doors were maps, pictures, articles, paintings, flags and any thing else that was related to Germany during the 1940's. Stacks of books lined one wall along with magazines and other printed material. Opening the closet in the bedroom, he found it filled with every German uniform that he could think of including one that reminded him of Hitler's complete with Jodhpur type trousers and tall leather boots. In a chest of drawers, he found grey uniforms with a company name across the left breast pocket.
    "Hey any of you guys know a Fenwick and Sons?" One of the deputies stepped forward and looked at the grey uniform shirt.
"The only one I know of is the funeral home and the cemetery."
    Stan looked at the young officer and grinned. "That explains the truck with the winch. Let's go visit this funeral home and see if they know who our Nazi is." He grouped every one together and told them to do an evidence procedure, picture's, bag and tag the entire works and to take it all to the cop shop and he would send an agent by later to collect all of it. Leaving with the deputy, they headed down the road to the funeral home and found the front door locked.
"Shit, now what?" Stan asked out loud.
"Sir the director lives in the house behind the funeral home, we can check there."

***

Rita and Marie stepped quietly into Rico's room, both

women smiled at the sight of the two younger women wrapped around each other. Soft snores came from both of them as they slept so tangled together that they couldn't tell where one started and the other ended. Rita wiped a tear from her eye and felt Marie squeeze her shoulder.

"They was meant fer each other, they balance between light and dark."

Rita looked to the older women with questioning eyes. "Light and dark?"

"Aye, they both have their demons to live with but between them, they can slay the demons and heal each other." She reached into her pocket and pulled out her wallet; searching through it she pulled out a picture and handed it to Rita. "It was taken a few weeks ago." It showed Shawn and Rico with their foreheads resting together and looking into each other's eyes. The connection between the two women was plan as day. "Feel happy fer wee bit, she's found what others haven't."

Rita looked to see Shawn snuggle deeper against Rico's chest; she had never seen her daughter look as peaceful as she did at that moment. "As long as she's happy that's all that matters." They were about to leave the room when Rico mumbled for Marie.

"Mama I'm hungry." Her pale blue eyes blinked a few times before she could focus clearly. "Uuhhm..."

"I'm Rita, Shawn's mom." She stepped closer to the bed and gripped Rico's hand gently. "You were sleeping last night when I was here." Rico started to panic when she felt Shawn move against her and run a hand up to cup her left breast in her small hand. A dark blush raced up her face when she saw Rita's brows bury themselves in her hairline. "She ahh..."

"I know all about my daughter's sleeping habits, just wait until she starts raiding the refrigerator in her sleep."

***

Stan and the deputy were able to track down the funeral director at a small diner down the street; it was not hard to locate the older man when they walked through the doors. He was the stereotypical pale faced creepy looking type that was always in the horror movies. When they approached the table, Stan showed him his identification and took a seat across from him.

"Mr. Fenwick can you identify this man for me?" He pulled a post mortem Polaroid from inside his jacket and held it out to the director.

"Looks like one hell of a barroom brawl did him in. Strange man he was, names Gerry Stone. Whenever I needed a grave dug or work done at the cemetery, I gave him a call. About three times a week, he would call in and see if I had anything for him. He was a free lancer." He took a sip of his coffee and raised his eyes up to Stan. "What did he do?"

"Let's just say that he didn't like a whole bunch of women." Stan stood up and shook the man's hand. "Thank you for your help sir." He grabbed his cell phone from his pocket and answered it as he walked out of the diner; he closed his eyes and replied to the person on the other end. "OK, be right there." Signaling to the deputy, he told him that they needed to go to the cop shop. They had found a map of the area that had all kinds of marks on it in different locations. He hoped that it was all the places that the killer had imprisoned his victims. Making a call to his office, he ordered all available agents and medical examiners to head out to the area to help search for the bodies. Knowing that he would have to make a visit to Rico, he planed on going over to the hospital after he picked up the map.

***

"You can't leave Rico!" Shawn said from where she was trying to block her lover from getting out the door. "You had surgery last night, a lung blow back up, you're covered in more gauze than king Tut and you have to get past me!"

A rough lopsided grin tried to form on her bruised and sore face. "Baby, I can and will get past you." Shawn's brows dropped down over her nose and then one brow rose to hang over a green eye.

"Baby? Did you just call me a baby?" She backed up and found herself pinned to the closed door by a scrub-covered body. A

105

moan rumbled in her chest when her lips were taken in a heated kiss. Wrapping her arms around her lover's neck, she leaned against her body for support. When the kiss broke, she waited a few seconds to catch her breath and open her eyes. What she found was an empty room and an open door. "Ohh you are in so much trouble!" She ran down the hallway and saw her lover wave to her from the closing elevator doors. "Still can't get away, you don't have a ride!" She yelled while racing to the door to the stairs that would take her to the bottom floor and where she hoped Rico would be heading. She was slightly winded as she burst through the stairwell door and caught sight of Rico going towards the side doors to the employee parking lot. She finally caught up with her as she was sticking keys into the door of a Toyota 4x4. She came to a sliding halt beside her lover and took her by her upper arm. "I am going with you and there's not a damn thing you can say about it!" She looked at the truck but didn't recognize it. "Whose truck is this?"

"No idea, I found the keys at the nurse's desk."

Green eyes widened at her. "What? You're stealing someone's truck! I don't believe we're doing this." She huffed and crawled across the seat and waited for Rico to get in. "Well what are you waiting for the cops?" They pulled out of the parking lot and headed for home, Rico wanted to get some clothes and get back out to the field. Granted, she felt like shit but she wanted to be out there when they searched the pit that she was kept in.

"Ya know when we get arrested and go to jail; I'm requesting a separate cell."

A dark brow rose over a blue eye. "Separate cell huh and why is that?"

"Because you're a bad influence on me." Shawn turned to sit sideways in the seat. "In one day, I've threatened flight attendants and CS agents, been chased by the police, drove without a helmet on, broke too many road laws to count, ran a guy over with my motorcycle, beat the shit out of him, shot him around 40 times and now I'm an accomplice to car theft. Now tell me you're not a bad influence."

"Well...I must say that you've got me beat in the breaking law department, I've only escaped from the hospital and stolen a truck. Sure ya want a separate cell; I'll make it worth your suffering." She wiggled her eyebrows.

***

Stan walked to the nurses desk and asked what room Rico was in, going up one floor, he walked down the hallway an opened the door to find it empty. Looking down the hallway, he saw Bobby coming his way.
"Where's Rico and Shawn, I have some news for them."
She gave him a bright smile and pointed ahead of him. "In that room in front of you."
"It's empty, are you sure she's not having tests or something done?"
"Ohh I'm sure, I would be the one doing them." She opened the door and came out seconds later with Rico's admittance bracelet and the gown she had been wearing. "Who ever catches them gets to kick both their asses!"
Stan ran from the hospital and flipped the flashing light and siren on before he pulled out on to RT. 9, cars pulled to the side of the road as he came upon them. An evil smirk covered his face as pedestrians jumped close the sides of buildings. He knew that him flying through the small town as he was had given them the most excitement since they put a stop light in town. Weaving around cars, he took the shortest way possible to Rico's house. They had to be heading home, where else could she go in hospital scrubs. Pulling his cell phone out, he called Rico's house and spoke to Marie. The last she had seen of her daughter and her tiny terror of a sidekick, they were at the hospital sleeping. He yanked the phone from his ear after he told her that they weren't at the hospital. What ever she was saying in Gaelic didn't sound like she was sending Rico and Shawn praises.

***

Rico pulled the truck onto a service road that ran beside her property. Turning it off she looked over to see a raise eyebrow above a green eye.

107

"What?"

"Exactly, why are we on this road and not the driveway?"

"Because if mama catches me, I'll end up back at the hospital having my ass reattached."

Shawn crossed her arms over her chest and tilted her head to the side; a smirk broke across her face. "And how does us being way over here keep your ass on?"

"Easy, we sneak up to the house; you crawl through our bedroom window…"

"Wooo there, I crawl through the window? Why can't you crawl through the window since this is your mission?"

"As I was saying, you crawl through the window." She gave her a charming smile before she continued. "Get us some clean clothes and then you change in the yard and I watch."

Shawn scratched her jaw, bit her bottom lip and then slugged Rico in her shoulder. "You need your head examined!" She threw her hands in the air and dropped her voice to sound like her lover. "And you change in the yard while I watch. NOT!

"Why not, it's the least you can do since I'm a recent surgery patient and can't have none; at least you can entertain me."

"Son of a…come on lets get this over with." She got out of the truck and started stomping off towards the cabin mumbling under her breath and throwing her hands in the air while the twinkling eyes of her very amused lover watched.

***

Shawn crept towards the window and went up on her tiptoes but couldn't reach the window to push it up. She planted her hands on her hips and turned to glare at Rico. Crooking a finger at her, she motioned her over and pointed to the close window. "Open." She whispered. Rico pushed the window up and stepped back to watch Shawn jump up and down trying to get high enough to get through the window. She bit down on her bottom lip to keep from laughing at her. "Damn it Rico." She went chin to chest with her and gave her a fiery look. "I can't fly through the window ya know."

"Damn and I was enjoying watching your ass flex." She took her over to the window, gave her a leg up and had to cover her mouth when she heard a yelp and something heavy hit the floor. She knew that the sound was most likely Shawn landing on her head. She waited and then clothes started flying out the window to land draped over her head and on the ground. Seconds later, Shawn appeared and dropped through to the ground below.

"You owe me wee one, big time!" She picked up some of the clothes and went back towards the truck. Before she could clear the trees, she heard her name being yelled by mama.

"Ahhh no ya don't, ya two gets yar asses over here!" She pointed to them and raised a fist in the air. "I oughta kick yar ass's good fer this." Rico dropped her head and dragged her feet across the yard; she lurched forward when she felt a foot connect with her   ass.
"Told ya you were a bad influence on me!" Shawn said as she pinched Rico on her ass and ran past her to hide in the cabin.

"Shoulda known it was yar idea wee one, black sheep that ya are." She took her daughter by her hand and dragged her into the cabin, the entire time she was speaking in their native tongue and what she was saying had Rico's face a deep red from embarrassment.

"Jed did what?" Shawn asked when she heard mama say something about Rico's boxers and the goat. She looked at her mom and turned as red as her lover. "Ohhh Gods, you saw us?" She covered her face when mama nodded her head.

"How did you two get here?" Mama asked.
"Uhhmm…we stole a truck." Rico mumbled.

"Jericho Mariah Chamaune what the hells wrong with ya? Where didja steals it from?"

Shawn gave Rico a funny look when her mother used her whole name; she knew her lover was in hot water now.

"From the hospital, it's OK though, Bridget won't mind."

Mama slapped her forehead and groaned, she knew that Bobby and Bridget would call the police and then it would hit them that Rico had taken it.

"How?" Was all mama said.

"I ahh swiped her keys from her pocket when she was

examining   me."
    "That's it!" Mama yelled. "Yar grounded to yar room,
now   get!"
    Rico's eyebrows buried themselves in her hairline, she
looked at a smirking Shawn. "Mama I'm 36 years-old!"
    "Going on two, now get!" Rico mumbled under her
breath as she walked past her lover, Shawn gave her a huge grin
that quickly disappeared when her mom pointed at her.
    "You to Shawna Maureen MacDonaill, go before I?" Was
all she got out before Shawn took off running after her lover.
    "Fix thar asses, make 'em sit and stare at each other."
Mama said and then thought of what they had just done. "Damn,
they be actin like rabid weasels!"

***

    Bobby and Bridget stood in the employee parking lot
looking all over the place for their truck. Bridget pointed to a spot
that now had a rusted out Ford Taurus sitting in her parking spot.
"I   swear   baby   we   parked   right   there."
    "Well it's not there now." Bobby spun her wife towards
her   and   started   searching   her   body.
    "I'm enjoying what you're doing but why are you doing
it?"
    "Your keys, where are your keys?" She pushed her hand
into Bridget's front pocket and pulled out a smashed pack of gum.
"Ewww now I know how our clothes get all nasty after they've
been washed." She tossed the gum over her shoulder.
    "A little to your left." Bridget moaned and turned her hips
trying to get the searching fingers where she wanted them.
    "Stop it this is not a search and please mission. No
wonder why you never noticed that you were being pick-
pocketed!" She pulled her hand out and smacked Bridget in her
stomach. "You   got   close   to   Rico   didn't   you?"
"Well…I did examine her this…damn her she did it again!"
They both turned when a set of flashing lights and the whoop of a
siren came from behind them. A tall sheriff leaned out of his
cruiser and waved to them. "I'll take you to mamas, she has your

110

truck."

"Just wait until I get my hands on Rico, I'm going to do a lower GI on her with a rotor rooter!" Bridget stomped off towards the cruiser with a smirking Bobby behind her.

**

Mama and Rita walked towards the front window of the living room when they heard sirens coming towards the cabin. A huge grin crossed their faces when they saw three pissed off faces and a grinning Sheriffs deputy striding towards the front door. Stan opened the door and waited for the other two women to precede   him. Mama pointed down the hallway towards Rico and Shawn's bedroom. "They been grounded ta thar room and all thar getting fer   supper   is   bread   and   water."

Stan was the first down the hallway; he covered his eyes and pushed the door open. "You two are in deep shit!" Two sets of eyes looked up at him in amusement from where they lay across   the   bed   facing   each   other.

"Gotcha Mariah!" Shawn placed her circle on the tic-tac-toe   square   blocking   Rico's   win. Stan uncovered his eyes and groaned he was expecting to catch them doing something other than playing games. "What in the Sam Hell is it with you boss, escaping the hospital and stealing a vehicle?" He sat on the foot of the bed and gave her a narrowed eyed   look.   "You   must   have   a   death   wish."

"Nope, have you ever eaten hospital food? Now that's a death wish." She rested her head on her hand. "What news have ya got for me?" He went on to tell her everything that they had found out including the topographical map that he had crumpled in his hand. He spread it out on the bed and showed them the red swastikas that were in different areas all over the map of the area that they had been searching for weeks. Shawn ran her finger up from the small dark line that was Rt. 340, across an open area, through the woods and to a spot that looked like it was in the middle of a large cluster of trees. She looked up with spooked eyes   to   her   lover.

"I think this is where I was, it has a lot of trees and that's what I remember. She looked to Stan. When can we go out and check it?" Stan was about to refuse her when he saw the flames erupt in her green eyes. Running a hand across his stubbled jaw, he cast a look at Rico. "Tomorrow morning that way I'll have a full force out there and I won't have to worry about you two getting into trouble. Which reminds me," He pointed a finger at Shawn. "You did not shot the Nazi, Rico did."

"No she didn't I...oohh I see what you're saying." She dropped her head to the bed and groaned. "Even if it was self-defense his family could press charges against me, not to mention that 40 bullet holes are a little bit of over kill. I could claim crime of passion, temporary insanity or post traumatic stress syndrome, but then we have the point of me running around pretending to be an FBI agent with two weapons that I'm not licensed to carry and..." She was stopped by a hand covering her lips.

"Wee bit how come you sound like a lawyer?" She pulled her hand away and gave her lover a questioning look.

"Damn! I just dropped to the bottom of the food chain because of my big mouth." She groaned and covered her head with her hands.

"Holly shit Rico, your girlfriends a lawyer!"

"Wait a minute here, you papers say that you were a linguistics student."

"I was...am, I was taking the class so that I could communicate better with all the different people that come through the prosecuting attorneys office. I'm one of the PA's in Dallas." She leaned up, reached down inside her shirt and pulled out Rico's badge. "Uuumm this is yours, Stan has your Glocks and shoulder harness."
A raised eyebrow from Rico made her roll her eyes. "So I was playing dress up, I always wanted to play cop and robber."

Rico pulled her close so that they were nose to nose, placing a soft kiss on her lips she whispered. "Just say the word and you'll have your own badge and guns."

"Excuse me? What are you getting at?"

"The FBI Academy in Quantico, you can go and become an agent." Rico looked over her shoulder at Stan and winked. He nodded   his   head   and   left   them   to   talk.

Shawn asked in between light kisses to her lovers face and neck. "Do I get to wear a dark suit and sunglasses, scare people, and get to visit the director in Tyson's corner?"

"I'm sure that the Stoic director could be convinced to let you visit permanently." She slipped a thick golden pinky ring from her finger and held it out to Shawn. "Will you make an honest   car   thief   outta   me?"

"Only if ya teach me everything you know." She held out her hand and felt the warm gold ring slid onto her finger. "I love you Rico." The sounds that came from their bedroom were not the screams of winning tic-tac-toe. They were so loud that everyone in the house went outside and sat at the back of mama's to be able to hear each other talk and not jump every time am inhuman roar pierced the air. Bridget looked to her wife and grinned   at   her.

"Sounds like mating season at the zoo, kinda familiar huh?"

Rita looked over at the couple and covered her ears, she didn't need the fact that her daughter was at that very moment having wild sex a few hundred feet away burned into her brain.

"I'm jealous as hell." Stan said from where he was leaning back in a lawn chair sipping a glass of mama's ice tea. "My FBI training was never like that." He slapped a hand over his mouth and gave everyone a wide-eyed look. "Ooppss…guess they should   have   been   the   ones   to   tell   you   all."

"My daughter is going to be an FBI agent?" Rita said with a stressed look on her face. "FBI Agent MacDonaill?" A wide grin broke across her face. "I like it, drinks are on me!" She jumped   up   and   ran   into   the   house. Mama knew more than what she would tell them, she looked at the remaining people and snorted. "Wonder what she'll think of havin the FBI Director as her daughter in-law?"

***

Bright an early the next morning Rico was hobbling around the kitchen looking for something to eat. With her and

Shawn's celebration, the night before neither one of them had wanted to leave the comfort of each other's arms to find food. Now with her stomach roaring and a slight lightheadedness from low blood sugar, she would eat anything as long as it didn't kick her ass before she killed it. Searching through the refrigerator, she found a container filled with potato salad. Grabbing two spoons, she was about to head back to the bedroom when the sound of 'maaa' came closer to the doggy door. In a blur of black and white, Jed ran past her. A loud yell came from the bedroom and then a squeaking noise. Rico snorted as she walked slowly towards the bedroom and watched Shawn try to hide under the covers as Jed was pulling on them. Rico felt a presence behind her and knew it was her mama when she felt her ass smacked.

"What is it with ya running around naked?"

"Why get dressed when I have to take a shower? Besides I like to tease wee bit."

"My daughter the exhibitionist, put yar robe on, Rita's coming over." Looking around her daughter, mama saw Jed playing queen of the bed by standing on Shawn's back. "Jed gets off her, yar just as bad as wee one, crawling all over her like that." Jed jumped off the bed and ran past them but not before stealing Shawn's shirt. Mama took the potato salad from Rico and gave her the raised eyebrow look. "Breakfast will be done in a few minutes, gets wee bit in the shower so ya can get out inta the field. And don't ya two spend all day out there." She jabbed Rico in the chest. "Yar in no condition ta be running around to begins with, having wild monkey sex right after surgery's bad enough. Surprised ya ain't dead this mornin."

***

Looking over the front seat of Stan's car, Shawn gripped Rico's hand tighter as they got to the fields, Stan had stopped by to pick them up so that they could get Rico's Blazer and Shawn's motorcycle. They both hoped that their vehicles were still there and in working order. Stan stopped his car at the edge of an area that would be to rough for him to drive further, they had used the coordinates on the map to get to where Shawn thought she had been held. They would have to walk the rest of the way and use a compass to keep heading in the right direction. Rico slipped her sunglasses on and winced when they put pressure on the bridge of her still sore nose. She had removed the bandages that morning and was finally able to see all the sutures that adorned her face. The worst gash ran from her left ear across her cheek to slop down towards the edge of her jaw. It would leave a thin scar but she wasn't worried about it. It would remind her that she had let down her guard. Shawn had decided not to have her scars fixed; she was going to have them covered by a large Celtic knot tattoo. As the three of them walked into the trees, Shawn's heart began to pound in her chest and her breathing became ragged. Gripping Rico's good hand, she could feel her lover's fingers getting cold from lack of circulation. "Sorry." She whispered as she let go of the larger hand and rubbed the fingers until they became warm again. "This is a little unsettling." Rico leaned down close to her ear and whispered.

"I'm here for you, if you don't want to go any further I'll understand."

Shawn stopped and turned to face Rico, her eyes showed a stern determination. "I have to do this, I have to face my demons and put it all behind me or I'll never be able to go on with it haunting my every waking moment." Wrapping her arms around her lover, Rico rested her chin on top of Shawn's crown.

"OK then, let's find this place and put everything to rest once and for all." After an hour of trudging through the trees and open fields, they looked like they were camouflaged, twigs and honeysuckle stuck in their hair, briars covered every inch that it could adhere to and they swore that their skin was crawling off their bodies. That could only mean that they were now vehicles for deer ticks. Stan tripped over an exposed root and fell to one knee, putting his hand down to push himself up, he yelled in surprise as his body fell forward leaving him face down in the tall grass.

"Son of a bitch!" He struggled to his knees and looked down into the hole. "Hey I found something here." He felt Rico come up behind him and look down into the dark hole, she looked over her shoulder into the terrified green eyes of her lover.

"Stan I think this was Shawn's escape tunnel, why don't you see if you can find that concrete slab." She walked back to Shawn and cupped her pale face with her good hand. "Wee bit, you don't have to go any further." Green eyes slowly focused on to blue, a fire began to rage in them and a deep growling noise rumbled in her chest. Memories flashed in her mind and rage filled her body to make it tremble. Without saying a word, she walked past Rico and right to where the concrete slab was.

"Give me the tag-along." She growled at Stan. He removed the backpack he had been carrying and held it out to her. Seeing that she was beyond talking to, he backed up to stand near his boss, in a low voice he asked. "Is she all right?"

"No, but she has to do this on her own." Shawn snapped the large hook of the tag-along onto the steel ring and released the cable until she was able to attached it to the closest tree. Hitting the locking mechanism down, she worked the handle until the cable became taught. Using her strong upper body, she forced the handle until she could see the slab moving a little bit.

"Rico that thing must weigh at least 1500 pounds, how the hell is she moving it?"

"Rage my friend, pure rage." She slowly walked over to her lover and placed a hand on top of hers, locking icy blue with fiery green, she nodded her head. Together, they worked the tag-along until the opening was a good three foot across. Shawn dropped to her knees and gasped for air. Her arms and back were burning from over exertion. Rico helped her to her feet and took her hand in hers before they approached the opening. The stench coming up from the pit made their stomachs roll and eyes water. Stan shined a flashlight into the hole and blanched, he could see the remains of the woman and bones littering the ground below. Pulling his cell phone, he asked for one of the medical examiners to be brought out to this area. He took a few steps away from the pit and saw that an open field was about 300 feet ahead of him. "I'll set off some smoke so you can find us." He closed the phone and groaned when Shawn dropped down into the pit. "Rico, what is she doing?" His answer was a shrug of wide shoulders. Shawn paced the small dark area; the rage was building hotter by the second. She could feel the fire coming from her stomach to swell in her chest. A low keening noise started deep in her stomach to grow louder as it worked it's way up to burst from her mouth in a howl. Flashes of the past ran behind her closed eyes, the pain she had been subjected to tore at her body sending her to her knees. Her fists clenched, arms shot out to her sides as she screamed out her emotional pain to the darkness. Long minutes past with her screams of rage until racking sobs over took her, tears flowed down her cheeks to drip from her jaws. She stood up on shaky legs and reached upward with one hand, her voice rough, she pleaded for help. Rico dropped to her knees, reached down, and grabbed her wrist, then she felt Shawn's other hand grab her wrist tightly. Taking a deep breath, she pulled her lover from the pit and into her arms. She sat back, pulled Shawn tightly against her body and let her racking sobs be absorbed into her own body. Tears flowed from her eyes to drip onto Shawn's shoulder where she rested her head. She could feel the internal pain her lover was going through. Leaning back, she lifted Shawn's chin and locked eyes with her. "I love you Shawn." She brushed her lips softly against her lover's. She felt arms wrap around her neck and the kiss deepen. Shawn felt a pale swirling light start deep in her soul, as it flowed upward into her chest it gained brightness until it erupted to blinding and burst forth to surround both of them in a shimmering aura. Their kiss broke leaving their breathing ragged and eyes locked upon one another. The connection they had felt remained intact and a new awareness passed between them. Stan stood at a distance from his friends and could swear that they had a light surrounding them. He put it off to exhaustion and stress. Tilting his head to the side, he heard the sound of a chopper approaching. Moving out into the field, he waited for it to land. As soon as the rotors stopped turning, he ran out to the pilot and told him to wait. Going back towards his friends, he kneeled down next to them and whispered into Rico's ear.

"The medical examiner is here, why don't you two take off and let them handle this?" Rico nodded her head, and stood up   with   Shawn   in   her   arms.
"We're going home, come by tomorrow and let me know

what you've got." Not waiting for an answer, she carried Shawn off into the trees and disappeared.

***

After getting a ride to her Blazer, Rico arranged for one of the agents to have Shawn's motorcycle delivered to the cabin. After her collision with the Nazi's body, the front forks were bent and the seals blown. It was nothing that couldn't be fixed in a matter of a few hours and new parts. They would have plenty of time to fix it now that everything was over. Once home, she carried a silent Shawn into their bedroom and removed her clothes. Locking eyes with her, she caressed her soft skin and then led her to the bathroom. Sitting her down onto the edge of the tub, she filled it with water and poured a small amount of sandalwood oil in, she quickly undressed and stepped into the tub and sat down and leaned back. "Come here wee bit." She held out her hand to her lover. When Shawn eased down into the water the scent of the oil soothed her, the feel of her lover's body wrapped around her brought calmness to her that healed her soul further. Sighing deeply, she caressed a strong forearm and rested her head back against Rico's shoulder.
"You know you shouldn't really be getting your incision wet or your   cast."
    "It'll be all right, I was going to cut the cast off tomorrow anyway." She kissed the side of Shawn's neck and murmured.
"Are   you   OK?"
    "As long as I have you I'll always be OK. I love you Rico." She turned and straddled her lover's thighs, cupping her bruised and battered face in her palms; she placed soft kisses over all the cuts and bruises. "Make love to me." With a gentleness, that Rico never knew she was capable of, she took Shawn to the precipice of ecstasy and held her there until she herself could not hold on any longer. They fell together screaming out each other's names as earth shattering orgasms ripped through them to leave them weak and gasping in the cooling water.

***

118

Shawn woke to find her self wrapped around Rico so tight that they could be Siamese twins. Pressing her lips between Rico's breasts, she grinned when sleepy blue eyes opened to gaze down at her.

"Morning wee one, sleep well?"

"Never better, how about you?" She ran her fingertips through sleep-tousled hair.

"No nightmares, but the feeling of…wholeness, does that make sense?" Shawn asked with a raised eyebrow.

"More than you know." She raised a small hand and kissed her ring finger and then all the others. Bringing her palm up to rest against the side of her face, she leaned into the warmth and sighed. Shawn tangled her fingers into long dark hair and pulled Rico's face down for a soul-searing kiss that left them hungry for more. Rico flipped Shawn onto her back and took hold of the soft skin of her neck and bit down hard enough to bring a whimper from her lover. Sucking deeply, she didn't let go until Shawn was squirming beneath her. Placing open mouth kisses downward; she latched onto a nipple and circled it with her tongue until it hardened to a taut peak in her mouth. Moving over to the other, she lavished it with the same attention.

"I'm gonna die Rico." She thrust her hips upward and felt a rush of warmth pour from between her lips. She tried to grind against her lover and growled when Rico moved out of range.

"No touching wee bit."

"What? You can't be serious." Her back arched and all words and thoughts left her when she felt a wet tongue travel down to her hairline. Dragging the tip of her tongue to Shawn's naval, she dipped it in with a slow frustrating tempo. "I'm going to…scream bloody…murder Rico!"

"Yes you will." Rico replied and then moved lower to tease swollen lips with the very tip of her tongue, to tease Shawn mercilessly. Tilting her head to the side, she French kissed her lovers womanhood. Shawn gasped and started a low rumbling moan as her hips thrust into Rico's devouring mouth. Her back arched and her body tightened like a bowstring, the muscles of her stomach rippled as her release came rushing forward to claim her. Her lover's name burst from her lips. She gasped when a hot tongue pierced her center and pushed deep inside of her sending her back over again. Rico used her middle finger and flicked Shawn's hardened clit, a loud scream pierced the air and hot juices flowed over her lips and chin. Licking the last of her lover's offering, she crawled up her sweat drenched gasping body to lie beside her and pull her into her arms. "I love you Shawn and I plan on showing you until we drop from exhaustion." Her body jerked forward when a small hand squeezed between their bodies to explore the soaking wetness that coated the insides of her thighs. Before she could take a breath, two fingers slipped between her nether lips and into her center. She rocked her hips against Shawn's hand.

"Come for me wee one." Shawn thrust her wetness against her lover's thigh to urge her on while breathing into her ear.

Rico took a shallow breath and stuttered. "Sha...wn com...ing!" Her head fell back as her orgasm twisted her body against her lover's. Shawn continued to pump her fingers inside of her clutching walls pushing her back up. Throwing her leg over Rico's hip, she thrust her center against her and felt it start to quiver at the same time her fingers were squeezed tightly signaling Rico's on coming second release. They came together with deep grunts and hot juices pouring from them to cover each other. After they caught their breathes, they fell into exhausted sleep with Shawn sprawled across Rico's body.

***

Mama and Rita crept through Rico's cabin; Stan had called her trying to get a hold of Rico. He said that her line had been busy for the last four hours and he needed to get a hold of her ASAP. Therefore, she and Rita decided to go on a search and reprimand mission of their daughters. Mama turned her head to give Rita an evil smile, she was enjoying herself immensely. Hell, she enjoyed anything that had to do with terrorizing her stoic daughter. If her agents realized that she was afraid of a little woman in her middle 50's they would never let her have a moment's peace. Stopping at the edge of Rico and Shawn's bedroom door, she held up a finger to her lips for Rita to be quiet. Peeking around the corner a huge grin came to her face at the two women sprawled naked across each other snoring up a storm. Waving to Rita, they walked into the room and took spots on either side of the bed. Mama flashed her friend a huge smile and pointed to Shawn's ring finger. Getting closer to Shawn, she ran a finger down her spine and then waited, she did it again and held back a snicker when Shawn sighed and squeezed Rico tighter. Changing tactics, she ran a finger from wrist to shoulder and then over to grab Shawn's nose. In seconds, green eyes popped open and her face turned beet red.

"Mama...ohh shit!" She dropped her head down onto Rico's breast and mumbled.

"And when exactly were you two going to tell us about this?" Rita leaned across the bed and wiggled her daughter's ring finger.

"Uhhmm after the fifth or sixth grandchild," Rico opened one eye and chuckled at the shocked looks on the older women's faces. "Just kidding unless one of us has a spit baby."

Mama planted her hands on her hips and snorted. "If that was the case wee one, the baby woulda drowned already the way ya go at it in here." She grabbed her daughter's big toe and pulled on it until it loudly cracked.

"Ooowwww mama!"

"So when was ya gonna tell us?"

"Now?" Shawn mumbled against her lover's breast. "Mom, mama I pissed off a lot of people, Rico's mine."

"Yeah ya pissed off Stan, he's been tryin ta get a hold of ya for the last four hours. Says the phones busy." She slapped Shawn's bare ass. "Says for ya ta gets your asses outta bed and get inta the office."

The older women left the room leaving their daughters to grumbling about having to get up when they were on vacation. "We're goin shopping so get a move on." Mama yelled back to them.

***

Dressed in faded Levi's, ratty T-shirt and black leather

chaps, Rico locked the helmets to the Indian and then took Shawn's hand in hers. After they were finished in the office, they were going to take a nice long ride out into the boonies. Giving Shawn a wicked grin, she let her eyes travel down across her body to the tight tank top that she wore. It showed off her strong muscular upper body to the point that Rico swore she could see her pectoral muscles flex as she walked. A rush of warmth washed through her body at the memory of their ride to her office. The press of firm breasts against her back and wandering little hands. She looked up to see a wicked gleam in her lover's green eyes and then the tip of her tongue peek out from between moist lips.

"Stop that." She bumped hips with her. "I'm hot enough after what you were doing to me."

"You said to hold on, but you never said where." Licking her lips and cocking an eyebrow. "It's not my fault that you just happen to have an irresistible body and I like to play with your nipples." She watched as a slight tremor went through Rico's body and she stumbled a step. "I'll hold on lower next time."

"Ohh I bet you will." Rico purred close to her ear and traced the outside edge with the tip of her tongue. A grin broke across her face at the gasp coming from Shawn. "The lower the better." She reached behind, cupped a tight ass with one hand, and then dragged her fingernails as far as she could reach down the back of Shawn's thigh. After she received the result that she wanted, she led her lover through the front doors and upstairs to her office. Few people were in the hallway unlike the other time they had been there. Going across the hall from her office, she pushed open the wooden door to see Stan leaning back in his chair with his feet up on the desk. He jumped when he saw his boss waltz in with Shawn, his eyes about popped out of his head at the way she was dressed. In all the years he had known her, never had he seen her look the way she did today. Electricity bounced between the two women and he could swear he heard it cracking. Her movements smooth and panther like as she stopped before his desk, lowered her sunglasses and looked over the tops of them with ice blue eyes.

"This had better be good to drag us out of bed."

Finding his voice, he croaked. "Rico its three o'clock in the afternoon, what were you two doing...never mind." He wiped a trail of sweat from his cheek. "It's good believe me, they found an old foot locker filled with driver's license, ID cards and all sorts of personal items." His eyes bugged when Shawn took off her sunglasses, her eyes were a light green with gold shooting through them. He knew that no one would last a heartbeat if she was to interrogate them. She could get the Pope to confess to the Lindbergh kidnapping with one glance. "It's in...your office." He stammered and took a deep drink of his cold coffee and choked. Pointing a finger at his door and wheezing. "Other...stuff...to." Rico gave him a grin that had his heart pounding in his chest, when she turned he saw that Shawn had her hand firmly stuck in the back pocket of Rico's Levi's. After his door had closed, he took a deep shuddering breath and dropped his head onto his desk. "Damn! Those are the two luckiest women on this earth!" He picked up the phone and called his wife to let her know that he was coming home early and to be ready.

***

"You are truly an evil person wee one."

Rico dropped her voice a few levels and purred close to her lover's ear. Yeah, but you love me anyway." Wrapping her arms around her lover, she pulled her up against her chest. "He's used to me being intimidating, I think it was you that gave him a hard on." She swooped down and captured Shawn's lips in a searing kiss. For lack of air and lightheadedness, they came apart. "Let's see what we have in the footlocker so we can get out of here."

Shawn took a ragged breath and nodded her head towards Rico's bathroom. "You look; I'm going to flush my head in the toilet for a few minutes." On weak legs, she walked to the small bathroom and closed the door. Leaning up against it, she dragged a hand down her face to her chest. Her heart was thudding so hard that she swore it would shot through her chest. Looking down, she saw that her nipples were so hard that they ached. When she took a breath, her shirt pulled across them and almost made her hit the floor on her knees. A coal furnace was burning between her legs so hot that she wouldn't need to shave her bikini line for a few months. "Don't think we'll make it to where ever we're going." She mumbled on her way to the small sink.

***

Rico looked through the box of papers on the floor next to the trunk and saw that they were clippings from a different newspapers and years. Leaving them for later, she pushed the lid up on the trunk and gasped. It was 3/4 of the way full of exactly what Stan had said. Taking a handful, she read some of the names and matched them to some of the case files that she had read numerous times. She would be able to close some of the missing person's cases and after the retrieval of the remains, the parents or loved ones could put closure to their lives as well. She didn't pay any attention when her office door was quietly opened and a soft click was heard when it was eased closed. She jumped when fingernails ran down the side of her neck, turning her head; she looked into the darkened eyes of Cassandra.

"I knew I could get a rise out of you if you gave me the chance." She stepped closer and brushed her lower body against Rico's stiff back. "I want to eat your pussy and make you come so hard that you pass out." She purred in a seductive tone.

A deep growling voice came from behind her. "I already do that for her numerous times during the day and night." Cassandra stiffened and side stepped away from Rico. Her eyes grew large as she looked into flashing light green eyes.

She crossed her arms over her ample breasts and lifted her chin. "I don't know who you are but this is a private office and a very private meeting."

Shawn threw her head back and let out a laugh that had the hair on her lover's arms stand up and wave. Dropping her chin towards her chest, Shawn bared her teeth and snarled. "Are you a slow learner or what Cassandra." She stocked towards her and had her backed up against the wall.

Cassandra's eyes showed fear; she looked to a smirking Rico and asked. "Aren't you going to help me?"

"Nope, I'm going to let my wife rip you limb for limb."

She gave her a bright smile, grabbed some stuff from the footlocker and took it over to her desk.

Cassandra's mouth fell open at the title Rico had used. "Wife? What, did you get rid of that skinny bitch you had in here the last time?"

Shawn grabbed her by the front of her silk blouse and walked her backwards towards the door. "I'm not a skinny bitch anymore, but I'm Rico's bitch. So if you have any brains in that head of yours Ca...la...ma...ri. You had better run for the nearest exit and never come near my wife again."

"It can't be, you look so..." was the last word she said besides the grunt when she landed in the hallway on her ass. Shawn closed the door, locked it and then slid a heavy cabinet in front of it. Rico looked up from her task and shot her an amused look.

"So much for fire regulations."

"The only fire in here is the one burning between my legs." Walking with a swing to her hips, she unfastened her Levi's and let them slip to her ankles leaving her naked from the waist down. Stepping out of them, she turned, gave her lover a sultry look before she sat on the edge of her desk. When Rico's mouth fell open, she swung her legs around so that she was looking out the window behind her lover's desk. Bringing her heels up onto the edge, she leaned back on her palms and waited. In a matter of seconds, Rico was squirming into her chair and pulling herself forward. Looking into sultry green eyes, she shuddered and then surrendered. Burying her face between Shawn's thighs, she moaned deeply against her sopping wet lips and breathed in her arousal. Using the flat of her tongue, she licked from back to front causing Shawn to let out a deep groan and thrust her hips upward. Placing Shawn's legs over her shoulders, she pull her as close as she could and devoured her essence until she fell back on the desk and shuddered her release. She lay with her eyes closed, gasping for air for long minutes. When she heard the scrounging noise of desk drawers being opened, she leaned up on her elbows and watched Rico pull a small black leather bag from the bottom drawer and place it on the side of her desk. Drawing the zipper back, she dumped the contents onto the desk and searched through the pile of sex toys.

"Wee one, play much?" Shawn asked and then picked up a purple vibrator.

"Actually no, I got these as Christmas presents from Stan and his wife. They were trying to tell me that I needed to get laid."

The little green head of jealousy monster popped up and slapped Shawn, her eyes narrowed and burned into blue. "Well did you...get laid?"

Blue connected and held with green to show complete honesty. "There's only been you in the last ten years."

Tears filled Shawn's eyes, both from feeling jealous and that Rico had closed herself off and been without companionship for so long. She sat up and cupped her lover's face between her palms, leaning forward she placed a soft kiss to her lips and pulled her head against her chest and held her. Kissing the crown of her dark head, she moved back and kissed her forehead. "I love you wee one."

"I love you to, more than you'll ever know." Rico was about to put the toys away when a small hand stopped her. Picking up a leather strap-on with a smaller knob inside the harness, Shawn ran her fingers across the lifelike shaft and grinned. Sliding down off the desk, she slipped the smaller end into herself, fastened the harness around her hips and then striped Rico of her chaps and Levi's. Grabbing her by her upper arms, she moved her so that she was sitting on the edge of her desk. Stepping between her legs, she ran a hand up the inside of her thighs and felt her wetness coating her skin. "Gods you're so wet and ready." Terror filled Rico's eyes as she looked down at the strap-on, lifting her eyes back up to her lover, she bit her lip and whimpered.

"What's wrong Rico?"

"It's just that...I've never..."

"Ohh Gods, I had no idea." She went to remove the strap-on but her hands were stilled.

"Wait...I want to try, just not here."

"OK, we can wait for some other time."

"No now, just not on my desk."

Shawn looked confused; she shook her head and ran her fingers through her hair. "Wee bit, come with me." She took her hand and led her to a bookcase. Moving a book, she pressed a button and the whole unit slid inward to reveal a small room with a twin bed against one wall, a nightstand and a large filing cabinet. Pulling Shawn into the room, she closed the opening and turned to her. "I had this built for when I can't make it home, plus I keep sensitive files in here." Lying down on the bed, she beckoned Shawn closer.

"Are you sure about this?" Her answer was Rico pulling her down on the bed and wrapping her long legs around her hips. Shawn kissed her with abandon, exploring every crevice of her warm mouth until they need to breathe. Cupping her breasts with both hands, she rolled her taut nipples between her fingers until she needed to feel her warm skin against her hands. In seconds, they had removed the final barriers and were so tightly pressed against each other that they became one. Finding the sensitive spot on her lovers shoulder, she sunk her teeth into her flesh and bit down hard enough to make Rico's hips thrust upward to make contact with the strap-on. A deep moan escaped her lips as she tried to make contact once again to find nothing. Shawn slipped a hand between them and coated her fingers with her lover's wetness. Leaning back, she rubbed the lifelike penis in an up and down motion causing more whimpers to come from a watching Rico. "I'll be gentle with you, I promise." Moving closer, she ran a finger across the hard bundle of nerves and watched her lover's center open to her. She felt her own juices flow out and run down her inner thighs. Bracing herself on her palms on either side of Rico's shoulders, she eased the very tip into her; she stopped for a bit and then pushed in a little farther. Pulling back out, she went in again slowly. She continued to do this until she felt long legs wrap around her hips, pull her in, and send the strap-on home. Rico's back arched up off the bed and a loud gasp rushed out. Slowly she moved her hips against Shawn until they had a rhythm going. "Harder!" Rico forced out between pants. Shawn pumped harder and felt her stomach tightened and all the nerve endings in her body scream out for release. Rico gripped her upper arms, her body tightened and she screamed out her lover's name and took her over the edge with her. Shawn collapsed on top of her, panting for air. She was going to pull out when Rico flipped her onto her back without loosing contact and straddled her hips. Leaning forward she nipped at her lower lip and when granted entrance, she filled her lover's mouth with a plunging tongue. Thrusting her hips downward, she rode Shawn until they climbed back up to the precipice and fell off. Collapsing to lay halfway across Shawn, they drifted off into a light slumber until a buzzing noise echoed in the small room. Green eyes shot open and looked around for the culprit who interrupted her sleep. "Tell me that I'm not hearing a damn buzz." Rico mumbled from where her face was buried between soft breasts.

"OK, you don't but I do. What is it?"

"Stan, it's connected into his office." She pushed herself up onto her hands and let out a low groan when she tried to remove the strap-on from inside of her.

"Don't move wee one." Shawn said as she grabbed a hold of her lover's hips. "Let me do this." She brushed her fingers across a sleep-wrinkled cheek. "You're tight and well..." She blushed at the smirk on her lover's face. "Well you are, but there's a trick to this."

A dark brow rose over a twinkling blue eye. "I'm all yours wee bit." Her body twitched when Shawn ran her hand down between them and teased her. Taking a nipple between her lips, she sucked and moaned against warm silky skin. When she felt wetness cover her fingers and Rico pump her hips, she slipped out of her to replace the strap-on with her fingers. Rico took the toy in her one hand and pumped it to match rhythm of the fingers inside her. Shawn's back arched and Rico's head fell back as they climaxed together. Before they could catch their breathes, the buzzer started up again.

"Mother fucking pain in the ass!" Rico growled as she moved backwards off the bed to stand on weak legs. "I'll kill HIM!" She stumbled from the small room, pulled her pants on and threw a suit jacket that had been hanging off the back of a chair on. Moving the cabinet and then yanking the door open, she stomped across the hall to her assistant's office. With death in her eye, she yelled "WHAT!" Stan nearly flipped over backwards in his chair. His eyes bulged at the sight of his boss's bare chest showing from between the lapels of her jacket. Clamping his hands over his eye's he stuttered.

"I was just wandering what you found in your research?" She leaned over his desk, pulled his hands down and gave him the most evil grin she had in her arsenal. "I found that my desk is an excellent place to have oral sex with my wife. Now stop interrupting my research!" She turned on her heel and stomped back out of his office leaving him feel tightness in his trousers.

"That's it, I'm going home!" He grabbed his briefcase, placed it in front of his crotch and walked on stiff legs out of his office. When Rico got back to her office, she found Shawn dressed and sitting on the floor by the footlocker.

"Did you kill him?"

"Nope but I think his hard on will. I watched him leave his office and he wasn't walking to good." Dropping down onto the floor next to her lover, she pulled her into her chest and kissed her gently. "He's got one erotic picture playing over in his head; I told him we had oral sex on my desk." Shawn's face turned ten shades of red; she dropped her head down to rest on Rico's shoulder. "I'll never be able to look him in the eye again."

"Yeah ya will, it's him that will be foaming at the mouth when he sees us." She kissed the crown of her head and then moved to sit cross-legged next to her. After hours of sorting through all the ID's and such in the foot locker, they had piles of them all sorted as to the kind of identification and by alphabetical order. Rico then printed up a list of all the missing women and they compared the list to the ID's. When they were finished, they had 250 names checked off. All that was needed now was to match the ID's to the remains found in the field. One case was solved already and that was the woman that had been in the pit with Shawn. Rico went to her computer and typed up a formal letter to the woman's parents, printed it and then signed it. Stamping "Case Closed" across the file, she set it to the side and leaned back in her chair with a sigh. Shawn came over, sat down on her lap, and snuggled into her body. They sat that way for a while before the sound of a roaring stomach brought them from

their   thoughts.
        "We can go down to the deli on the first floor and get
something   to   eat   if   you   want?"
        "Oohh I want all right, I need my strength for later."
        "What's later?" Rico asked her wife when she got up off
her   lap.
        "Bedroom romping contest," She pointed a finger at her
wife. "That has got to go. You're not going anywhere until you
put   your   shirt   on."
With an innocent look, Rico flipped the sides of her suit jacket
open. "You're no fun." She let the jacket slip from her shoulders
and land in her chair. "Could go like this and watch you beat the
shit   out   of   everyone   in   the   deli."
        "Maybe another time, I'm drained right now."

                            ***

        A few days later and after spending hours breaking in all
the toys they had brought home from Rico's office, they sat side
by side at Rico's PC staring at the screen until their eyes were
crossed. Shawn was the first to rub her eyes and give up for the
night. The reports on the remains had been trickling in a few at a
time and now it was part of Rico's job to collect the information
and then close the cases. They had hit most of the states and were
not even close on solving all of them, but they were closer and
knew that some of the loved ones could put things to rest. She
had sent out E-mails to some of the police stations where the files
had come from and told them of what they had discovered there
and that they may want to check the surrounding areas for the
same thing. The personal items from the man's hotel room had
been handed over to a profiler to study and add the information to
the computer base to help with other cases that were similar.
Giving up for the night Rico leaned back in her chair and
stretched out her stiff neck and shoulder muscles. Getting stiffly
from her chair, she took Shawn's hand in hers and led her to their
bedroom. They undressed and crawled into bed and into each
other's arms. "Do you mind if we don't romp tonight?" Shawn
asked through her yawn.

"No I don't mind, I just want to snuggle." Those were the last words Rico uttered before a light snore came from her parted lips and lulled Shawn in to sleep with her.

***

Mama and Rita were at the kitchen table; Jed was running around it and down the hall and back again with one of Rico's pairs of boxers in her mouth. They hadn't seen too much of their daughters lately because they had been locking themselves away in the small office. Between meals, they were able to terrorize the gist of the cases out of them and were happy that it was almost over. Rita had yet to have the chance to talk to Shawn about her own future; it was something that she didn't know how Shawn and Rico would react when she told them. Playing with the small royal blue box on the table, she looked up into blue eyes and smirked.

"Think they'll be mad?"

"Ahhh ta Hell with 'em, it's our lives not theirs." Mama spun a small box on its corner and watched until it lost momentum and fell flat. At the sound of shuffling feet, they both looked up to see two half-awake and dressed women come into the kitchen. Neither one of them knew what to do about them and their problem with wandering around half-naked. Shawn wore the light PJ top that matched the bottoms that Rico wore. This would not be a problem if she wore a shirt with it. Rita had gotten over her embarrassment weeks ago, now it was quite normal to catch them sometimes doing strange things to each other. At least they were strange to her. Rico dropped down into a chair across from her mama, her eyes mere slits, face puffy and pale white lines scattered her bronzed face from the healed cuts and gashes. A low grunt came from her when Shawn dropped onto her lap and snuggled her face against her neck. A soft snoring and grumbling came from the small women as she fell back to sleep.

"Ya two look like shit, ya need a day off from being in yar office."

Yawning and rubbing her eyes, Rico mumbled loud enough for the older women to hear but not wake Shawn. "We're

131

almost done, a few more days and all the results should be in."

"Well, today you two are taking off. We have plans and no one is going to ruin them." Rita pointed a finger at the tall woman she now thought of as her other daughter. Her green eyes shot over to her friend to wink at her.

"Yep, now wake up wee bit, we have something for ya and ta tell ya." Rico's heart slammed in her chest, she finally noticed the small boxes in front of their mothers. The entire short conversation had her mind spinning in circles. Her eyes now wide open she looked to her mama. "What are you talking about?"

"Not until wee bits awake, don't wanna have ta repeat it over again."

Rico whispered close to her wives ear and ran a finger across her parted lips. After a few nips to her ear, she opened her eyes to glare at Rico. "Love ya later, sleep…five minutes."

A loud snort came from mama. "Ya little pervert no sex at the kitchen table."

"But we've…never mind." She blushed and hid her face against Rico's neck. Rico found the tabletop interesting after seeing raised eyebrows from her mama and Rita. Mama slid one of the boxes across the table to Shawn and Rita did the same to Rico.

"We know that ya can't be married legally, and ya two haven't gotten around ta doin anything about showin the world. Well except for us that is." She looked to Rita to finish.

"So we took it upon ourselves to help you two out." Giving them a bright smile, she pointed to the box. "That's from me to you Rico and the other one is from Marie to Shawn."

Both women with hesitant movements opened the boxes and found thick wedding bands of gold. In silver was the word intertwined in the center of the band. Two sets of eyes filled with tears as they slipped the rings onto each other's fingers. Shawn slipped the original ring that Rico had given her back on so that she now wore both rings. Taking Rico's larger hand in hers; she placed a kiss on the ring and then her lips. "Now we're complete." They got up from the chair and had a group hugging and crying session in the kitchen until they heard voices yelling their names.

Seconds later, Jed came barreling into the kitchen with Shawn's bra in her mouth, Bobby, and Bridget behind her carrying huge trays of food. Seeing the four women hugging each other, the new arrivals joined them. When they all broke apart, Bridget wrapped herself around Rico and planted a wet slobbery kiss on her   cheek.

"I always wanted to do that." She chuckled at the shocked expression   on   her   friends   face.

Shawn cleared her throat and gave Rico a funny look. "I don't think she meant kissing you either, go put a shirt on."

"Only if you put pants on," Rico said while walking past everyone to come to stand in front of her wife. "That is if Jed hasn't dragged them outside." Taking her hand, she led her to their   bedroom.

"Ya gots five minutes to gets back out here; we didn't set this all up fer ya ta goes in there and play with all those sex toys." Mama busted up laughing when she heard Shawn say, "You told her?"

***

Everyone sat outside after filling their stomachs to the point of pain, with the exception of Shawn who was still eating the remainders off Rico's plate. They all turned their heads when Stan came out the back door with a thick envelope in his hand. Shrugging his shoulders, he handed it to Rico and gave her a small grin before connecting with green and turning beet red. "I got the last of the results and compared them to the list you sent me. All the other names have been placed in the computer for other agencies to see. It's just a matter of time before the rest of them are closed." He pointed to the envelope. "Open it, it concerns   both   of   you."

Rico cocked an eyebrow at him and opened the envelope, inside were papers signed by the head of the FBI saying that Shawn had completed certain courses and would only need to attend the FBI Academy for weapons training and some other classes, the time totaling one month. Another paper stated that her office would be at Tyson's Corner and her immediate boss would be Rico.

"Stan how in the hell did you do all this. It's never been

done   as   far   as   I   know."

"Well...I got copies of her college transcripts, law degree and everything else I could get. Ran her forged application through to the top with a recommendation signed by you giving her credit for the cases that you two closed and with in a few days the   big   guy   called   me   and   gave   me   those."

Shawn's eyes grew large. "You forged our names?"

"Yep, I sign Rico's all the time." He knew he said too much when blue eyes glared at him. "Well...since you've been gone I have." Shawn got up, gave him a hug, and kissed his cheek.   "Thank   you."

"No problem, glad to have you aboard. Maybe you can keep the boss there in line. Gods know no one else can."

"Will someone tell me what the hell is going on and what's this about the Academy?" All eyes turned to see Bobby and Bridget standing with arms crossed over their chests.

"Ohh that's right you guys didn't know." Shawn gave them a big grin. "I'm giving up being a prosecuting attorney to become a FBI Agent. You'll be there for my graduation next month   won't   you?"

"Hold on there Shawn, you won't be around until next month." Stan pulled an envelope from his pocket and handed it to her. She opened and fell into Rico's arms. Inside were six tickets to   Ireland   and   six   returning.

"Stan?"

"Hey, it's the least I could do. This is the happiest I've seen   Rico   in...ever.   Go   and   enjoy   yourselves." Rico looked at the tickets and saw that there was no return date on them. She wondered why there were six of them and what her friend was up to.

"Stan, who all did you plan this for and why no return date?"

"Ohh sorry, my over sight." He stepped back and pointed to the six women. "You're all a part of this, all intertwining with each other's lives in some way. So we all thought you should all have a vacation together. I know you're gonna ask so I'll tell ya now. I took up a collection at the office for your honeymoon. Everyone gave something just too...get rid of you for a while." He gave her a huge grin and laughed at the way she slumped down in her chair. "Just kidding, they are happy for you guys and wish you luck."

"I've got something to say here about all this." Rita stepped forward and stood in front of her daughters. "When we come back, I'm not going back to Texas." Taking a deep breath, she continued at a lower tone. "I'm moving in with Marie." Shawn and Rico looked between their mothers and nodded. "OK, fine with us right wee bit." Shawn shook her head and smiled.

"Fine with me to, but you keep Jed in your own bedroom. Damn little hooves hurt like hell when she jumps on ya."

Mama looked to Marie and shook her head. "Damn nosey kids." She took Marie's hand and they walked off towards her house.

Rico eyed the older women then swung her disbelieving eyes to her wife. "Did I miss something here?"

"I think we all did." Shawn ran back over what she had said, and then the replies from mama and her mom. "You don't think they're...you know..."

Bridget offered them a toothy grin."Having geriatric aerobics classes in mama's bedroom?" A lot of mumbles and other grossed out noises came from the small group at Bridget's remark. Stan left for home leaving the women to sit around and ponder what could be going on between Marie and Rita. Four sets of eyes stared at the house a few hundred feet away and all they could see was the living room light shinning through the shear curtains and Gaelic music blasting from the open windows. As it grew to dusk, they still sat staring at mama's house.

"Are we on stakeout?" Bobby asked in a whisper.

"Huh? Rico asked without moving her eyes from the shadows now visible through the pale light in the house.

"Are we staking out the moms? You know like you used to do on cases." Bridget bounced a beer cap off Rico's head trying to get her attention.

A low chuckle shuddered from Shawn, she tapped her lover's thigh and pointed to where a small black and white body was running from the back door, seconds later a scantly clad Rita and mama went out the door after her. Stopping in mid stride,

Rita saw them being watched. She grabbed mama by her hand, pointed and they both ran back in the house.

"Uhhmm…" Rico turned her wide blue eyes to Shawn.

They all jumped up from their seats and went chasing after Jed; Bobby dove after the screaming animal and grabbed the item that was hanging from her small mouth. Lying on her back in the grass, she looked at what she had in her hand, screamed and threw it at her wife. It went back and forth between the two of them until Rico snagged it in mid air.

"I guess this answers our question." She handed a latex dildo with leather harness to Shawn and smiled. "Just think we can all join the mile high club on the way to Ireland."

***

One year later, there were now three houses on the property. Bobby and Bridget built a house next to mamas; now they had their own little community started. Shawn continued to work at the Tyson's corner FBI office under the watchful eyes of her temporary boss Stan while Rico took some time off. Wearing a dark Armani suit and dark sunglasses, she walked through the cabin to find everyone lounging around the in ground heated swimming pool. Rico lay stretched out in a reclining lawn chair with a towel draped over her stomach while everyone else was in the pool laying on life rafts. Sitting on the edge of the chair, Shawn pulled back the towel and placed a gentle kiss on her wives swollen stomach. She had just one more week before her due date; she couldn't wait until it was over. If she decided to get pregnant again, she would plan so that she didn't have to be as big as a house in the middle of the June and July months. "Love you little bit." Shawn whispered against warm skin and smiled when she felt a little kick. Sliding her sunglasses up to rest on top of her head, she moved up to capture parted pink lips in a soft kiss. A low mumble came from Rico's throat as she was pulled from her nap. "Love you mommy." Shawn kissed her deeper and moaned when a hand reached inside her jacket and caressed her breast through her silk shirt. "Bed now." Was all Rico said, she struggled to get herself out of the recliner and was pulled up by

Shawn's strong hand on her upper arm. "Rico we can't do that, you're to close to your delivery date." Shawn whined. Rico pulled her reluctant wife into their cabin and rushed her into their bedroom. Stripping her of her clothes with haste, she backed her up until she fell onto the bed. Rico then removed the few clothes she had on and crawled across Shawn to lay on her back in the middle of the bed. "Ricoooo, as much as I want to make love to you…" A large hand clasped over her mouth and stopped her whining.

"Wee bit, I can't but you can. I've been thinking about you all day, I'm so damn horny that I'm going insane!" Her eyes were a deep blue and Shawn knew that a sexually frustrated Rico was hell on wheels.

"How is you getting me off going to help you?"

"Because, that's what I want."

Shawn gave in and crawled up the bed to straddle her wives face, gripping the headboard she looked down into happy blue eyes. With the first feel of a warm wet tongue slipping between her nether lips, she jerked her hips and moaned. It always amazed her how fast she got wet and ready around her wife, with one touch of her tongue she was over flowing with juices and ready to climax within seconds. Her hips thrust back and forth to match the rhythm of her wife's tongue, every nerve ending was singing for release. The second she felt fingers slip inside of her, she let out a yell and shuddered her release and felt Rico gasp out against her with her own. Dropping her head down onto the headboard, she took deep calming breathes.

"Shawn…we…have a…problem." Rico forced out as her hips thrust upward. "I'm wet."

Shawn moved so that she was lying beside her panting wife and caressed the sweaty hair from her face.

"I'd hope so or I'd be worrying about us."

Rico took her hand and placed it on the bed. "I'm very wet and so is the bed. My water broke." Shawn's eyes grew wide; she scurried off the bed and pulled on her clothes. She ran in circles looking for her shoes and was near hysterics when she couldn't find them.

"We have to get you to the hospital!" She dropped to the floor and was about to crawl under the bed when she heard Rico's voice above her.

"Wee bit, we have a doctor and a nurse by the pool French frying their bodies."

Shawn's head popped up along side the bed; she pointed a finger at Rico. "Right! Be back." She ran to the door and came to a sliding halt, ran back to Rico and kissed her deeply. "Don't do anything!" She ran for the door and down the hall screaming for help.

"This is going to be...oohh geez...fun!" She gasped when a contraction ripped through her body.

***

"Hurry little bit coming!" She ran around the pool jumping up and down and pointing to the cabin. "Rico...water broke...baby!" She kept stuttering until mama grabbed her and made her calm down.

"Shawn what the hell are ya babbling abouts?"

"Baby coming NOW!" She dragged mama towards the cabin, stopped and ran back to grab Bridget. "Help! Boil water, get towels!" She babbled.

"Knock your ass out!" Bridget yelled as she pushed Shawn towards mama and went to her own house to get her medical bag. "Come on Bobby, we got a little bit to bring into this world." When everyone got into the bedroom, Rico looked like her head was about to spin and pea soup spew from her mouth. Her voice deep and threatening, she pointed to Shawn. "YOU COME HERE!" Shawn tried to run from the room but was caught by her mom and pushed backwards towards Rico.

"No you don't, you got her pregnant now you suffer the pain with her."

"Mom! I hate pain and she's gonna hurt me." Her voice dropped a few octaves. "Real bad!"

"No more than I will, now get up there and hold her." Shawn crept to the bed and eased behind Rico, lifting her up to a slight sitting position, she placed her hands on her swollen stomach.

"Is this OK?" She asked in a whisper. She felt Rico push back against her and let out a low grunt with another contraction.

Bridget crawled up between Rico's legs, bent her knees and spread her legs wider. Wiggling an eyebrow at her, she made a smart-ass remark. "Mizz Rico, I don't know nothin about birthin no babies."

"You…better learn…fast. Ohhh shit!" She gasped out and bore down with another contraction.

"I see something here, Bobby hand me a towel and the forceps." Bobby came to stand beside her wife while mama and Rita stood behind Bridget with their arms wrapped around each other. They had been thrilled when their daughters told them that Rico's favorite cousin was willing to be a sperm donor for them. They had the sperm flown back to the states where a doctor Bridget knew did the artificial insemination with Shawn's eggs and then transplanted the eggs into Rico's womb. Because of being raped so many times, they were told that Shawn would be risking her life as well as a baby's if she got pregnant. The doctor didn't know if she would be able to carry full term because of the scaring on her cervix if they wanted to take the chance. They decided to do it this way, and then the baby would be both of theirs. Rico gripped Shawn's thigh with one hand, brought her arm up and latched onto it with her teeth right before the next contraction hit her. Shawn let out a blood-curdling scream and didn't stop until Rico's body relaxed a little. Every one in the room was wincing from the scream she let out. Taking Rico's hands and holding them down on her thighs, she gave them a little squeeze. "Thanks wee one, I always wanted something to remind me of you every single day." She looked down at the deep purple mark on her forearm with the perfect impression of her wife's teeth.

"Glad I could help."

"OK, Rico on the next one I want you to give it all ya got." Bridget patted her knee and grinned. "Almost crowning now." Bobby handed Shawn a towel to wipe Rico's face with and gave her a softened look, she and Bridget may never have children but they would be the best aunt's they could to Rico and

Shawn's little one. "You guys are doing great." She said before giving Shawn's shoulder a squeeze. Shawn felt Rico push back against her, watching as her stomach seemed to roll and then every muscle in her body tensed.

"Ohhh son of a BITCH!" She screamed out, panted and screamed again as another strong contraction hit.

"OK Rico, we have a crown. Couple more pushes and you're done."

"I'm done now." She whimpered and cried against Shawn's shoulder. "So tired." Shawn wrapped her arms around her and kissed her temple.

"Almost done wee one, you can do this." She offered her arm to her. "You can bite me if you want." She heard a soft chuckle and then Rico tensed against her and screamed.

"We have shoulders girls, one more big push Rico."

Ice blue eyes narrowed and drilled into Bridget, a low snarling noise came from bared teeth, gasping she threw her head back and screamed.

"FUCK ME!" And then collapsed back against Shawn. Her eyes closed and breathing heavy, she lay unmoving and exhausted.

"Shawn all ready did that. Uhhmm well if I'm not mistaken we have a wee bit here." Bridget held up their daughter to show everyone. Bobby clipped the forceps onto the umbilical cord and handed Shawn the scissors. "It's all yours Shawn."

Wide green eyes looked to Bobby. "I can't...I..." She felt Rico's hand come to rest on her forearm.

"You can do it wee bit." Shawn took a deep breath a cut the umbilical cord and then watched as Bobby tied it. Wrapping the baby in a towel, she handed her to mama and let her and Rita take her into the bathroom to clean her up. Bridget motioned to Bobby, when she got closer, she whispered into her ear. Running her hand across Rico's stomach in a soothing motion, she waited for Bobby to get the items she needed. Shawn noticed something being very wrong; Rico was just lying against her and was passed out, her heart started to beat out of her chest with fear.

"Bridge what's wrong?"

"Nothing really." She tried to hide her worry from showing in her eyes. "I just need to suture her, she has a tear and it's bleeding to heavy for my likes."

"She's going to be all right isn't she?" Just then, Bobby came rushing back into the room with another medical bag and a bag of clear fluid. Taking an intro setup from the bag, she moved to Rico's side and prepared her arm for the intravenous needle. Slipping it in, she attached the tubing from the IV bag into the shunt in Rico's arm and then injected a syringe of oxicin into it.

"OK Bridge, she's all set."

"I need both of you to hold her legs apart so that I can suture her up.

Shawn eased out from under her now unconscious wife and moved to the side of the bed. Holding onto Rico's leg, she moved it so that Bridget could work easier.

"Let's wait for the after birth to release first." She massaged Rico's stomach for a few moments and watched as her muscles contracted and the placenta began to be pushed out. When she heard a loud thump, she looked to see Shawn flat on her back on the floor and out cold.

"Uuuhmmm MAMA!" Bridget yelled and started chuckling. "Just like a man."

***

Rico lay with one arm around Shawn and the other holding Sammy as she nursed at her breast. Shawn had yet to wake up; Bobby said that her being so stressed had a lot to do with it. She was just glad that she hadn't been awake to watch Bridget suture Rico's torn cervix. With women Rico's age, it was common for the cervix to not have the elasticity that it would in a younger women. When she gave birth, the cervix tore away from the uterus causing her to hemorrhage. Placing a kiss on her daughter head, she turned her face to nuzzle Shawn's neck. "What a big tough FBI agent you are wee bit." She kissed the side of her neck and smiled when she heard a soft sigh and her arm squeeze her gently. Green eyes peeked open and slammed shut again. "I saw that wee bit, come up here and meet our little girl."

"But I'm a wuss." She whimpered.
Rico chuckled and kissed her forehead. "No you're not; you're a very sensitive person."

Shawn leaned up on her elbow and snorted at her wife. "Nice way of saying I'm a wuss." Kissing Rico's lips softly she whispered against her lips. "I love you mommy."

"Love you to daddy." She broke out laughing at the look on her face. "Sorry, it's Bridget's fault. She said you acted like a man."

"S'kay, I can be the daddy and teach her how to fix cars and stuff." She ran her fingers through the soft blonde hair of their baby; tears of happiness filled her eyes. Their baby was healthy and Rico was OK.

"You guys know that Shawn had blonde hair when she was a baby." Rita said from the doorway with mama standing next to her. "What me and mama want to know is what color the nameless one's eyes are?"
Both Rico and Shawn caught the nameless part.

"Wee bit?" Rico smiled when Shawn nodded her head. "Samantha Brennan MacDonaill-Chamaune's eyes are..." Shawn leaned in close to peer into the baby's eyes; a bright smile came to her face as more tears flowed down her cheeks. "The same color as her mommy's, a beautiful ice blue." They had decided to name her after Rico's brother as a remembrance that with each death a new life comes forward. They had kept their choice a secret from the others so that they could surprise mama. The pitter-patter of little hooves announced the entrance of Jed with her sidekick Bridget's ugly little beagle and hairless Chihuahua mixed dog, Bridget's ugly goat or Bug as everyone called her, followed by Bobby and Bridget.

"The evil aunts are here, where's our niece?" Bobby asked as she looked over mama's shoulder. "Time to spoil her rotten and turn her against everyone."

***

Sammy was with Bobby and the others so that Rico could

rest. Shawn still a little afraid of leaving her alone lay wrapped around her refusing to let go. She had never dreamed of having a life as she did now, she had a loving wife, new baby and an extended family. As much as she hated to think about the past, she knew that if the psycho had never kidnapped her, she would never have met Rico. Lifting up onto one elbow, she turned Rico's face to hers and brought their lips together in a loving kiss. Her heart slammed into her chest when Rico took her hand and slipped the wedding bands from her finger and cupped them in her larger hand, and then slipped hers off and handed it to Shawn. "Rico what are you doing?"

Rico turned onto her side and gazed with loving eyes into terrified green orbs. "This is something we should have done a long time ago. I never knew that I could be this happy. You make my life complete and fill me with so much love, that at times I feel like I'll explode. I love you Shawn." She slipped the rings back on to Shawn's finger and placed a kiss on them as she had in the past.

Shawn wiped the tears from her eyes; she had never heard her wife say things like those that she had just said. Clearing her throat, she took Rico's larger hand in hers and ran a finger around the white area on her ring finger. "I'm the luckiest woman in the world; a long time ago I thought my world had come to an end. I was surrounded by darkness and knew that, at any minute I would be extinguished like a flame. Even when I escaped, I didn't know what would happen to me. I was in a strange place and still fearing for my life." She kissed the palm of Rico's hand and brought it up to press against her cheek. "Then out of the darkness came the sweetest voice I had ever heard, singing a song in my own language. Then a pair of the bluest eyes I had ever seen pulled me in and held me safe. You are my savior, what makes my soul peaceful and chases away the darkness with just a thought. I love you Jericho." After she slipped the ring on to her finger, she brought their lips together in a deep love filled kiss that sealed their lives together for eternity. After long moments they came apart to stare into each other's tear filled eyes.

Rico caressed her cheek with her fingertips and gazed into light green eyes. "Well Special Agent MacDonaill-Chamaune, I know that we're both lucky because we have each other, Sammy and a bunch of baby sitters." Kissing her forehead, she rested her head on Shawn's shoulder. "But it gets better?"

"How's that?"

"Bobby's pregnant."

A wide grin came to her face. "And we get to be rotten aunts?"

"Better, Bridget doesn't know yet."

"Huh? How can she not know?"

"Because she just took the test an hour ago and..." THUMP!

They looked to the doorway and saw Bridget lying on the floor.

"Guess we're in trouble huh?"

Rico jerked the blankets up over their heads. "Only if she finds us that is." Hysterical laughter was heard coming from the master bedroom, but with every ones attention on the new addition to the clan, no one cared.

For those who came to visit the women, would swear that they traveled back in time to Ancient Greece. With the seven females, living in a small communal type environment, made visitors think of a new Amazon Nation set in the middle of Virginia.

The End

Order These Great Books Directly From Limitless, Dare 2 Dream Publishing

Cat on the Couch by Cathy L. Parker	16.00	Hilarious
Kara: Lady Rogue by j. taylor Anderson	15.00	Adventure
The Amazon Nation by C. A. Osborne	15.00	Reference
A Woman's Ring by Rea Frey	16.00	NEW
Sweet Melody by Liana M. Scott	16.00	NEW
Deadly Rumors by Jeanne Foguth- OUT OF PRINT	15.00	VERY Limited
Walnut Hearts by Jackie Glover	17.00	NEW
Soldiers Now by Dean Krystek	16.00	November 2004
Home to Ohio by Deborah E. Warr	15.00	Mystery
The Mysterious Cave	12.00	Children's Adventure
Where Love is Not by Deborah E. Warr	16.00	NEW Ellen Richardson Mystery
		Total

South Carolina residents add 5% sales tax.
Domestic shipping is $3.50 per book

Visit our website at: http://limitlessd2d.net

Please mail orders with credit card info, check or money order to:

Limitless, Dare 2 Dream Publishing
100 Pin Oak Ct.
Lexington, SC 29073-7911

Please make checks or money orders payable to **Limitless**.

Order More Great Books Directly From Limitless, Dare 2 Dream Publishing

Seeds of Thorns by Marie DeLardi	17.00	July 2004
Lycanthropy: The Pack by Daniel Ellis	16.00	July 2004
So Close, So Far by Nikki Grin	16.00	July 2004
Time and Time Again by Nikki Grin	16.00	July 2004
Forever Autumn: A Love Story DeeAnn Burnette-Lundquist	16.00	July 2004
Strange People, Scary Stories by William Talmon Harbour	18.00	Short Stories
The Dark One by Bill Purcell	17.00	Aug 2004
Romping Joyously Towards Cronehood by Heidi Brinckerhoff	16.00	June 2004
Two Cats on the Couch by Cathy L. Parker	16.00	July 2004
The Broken Brain by Cathy L. Parker	16.00	July 2004
Perpetual Guide-Numerology by Debra Theissen	16.00	NEW
		Total

D2D Baseball Caps now available for $14.95 each
Plus shipping and Handling

South Carolina residents add 5% sales tax.
Domestic shipping is $3.50 per book
Please mail orders with credit card info, check or money order to:

Limitless, Dare 2 Dream Publishing
100 Pin Oak Ct.
Lexington, SC 29073-7911

Please make checks or money orders payable to **Limitless**.

Order These Great Books Directly From Limitless, Dare 2 Dream Publishing

Humanz by Richard Ellis	17.00	SciFi-NEW
Pirate Justice:Kara's Story by j. taylor Anderson	17.00	Adventure-NEW
Poetry from the Featherbed by pinfeather	17.00	Poetry
A Woman's Ring by Rea Frey	16.00	NEW
Sweet Melody by Liana M. Scott	16.00	NEW
Still Life by Tracy Haisley	17.00	NEW
Walnut Hearts by Jackie Glover	17.00	NEW
Soldiers Now by Dean Krystek	16.00	November 2004
Sins of the Innocent by Deborah E. Warr	18.00	Mystery-NEW
Guardians of the Stone by Josiah Lebowitz	17.00	SciFi/Adventure NEW
Where Love is Not by Deborah E. Warr	16.00	Ellen Richardson Mystery-NEW
		Total

South Carolina residents add 5% sales tax.
Domestic shipping is $3.50 per book

Visit our website at: **http://limitlessd2d.net**

Please mail orders with credit card info, check or money order to:

**Limitless, Dare 2 Dream Publishing
100 Pin Oak Ct.
Lexington, SC 29073-7911**

Please make checks or money orders payable to **Limitless**..

Printed in the United States
25100LVS00005B/152

9 780976 076933